CAT CIRCUS

Benjamin in the shopping bag

CAT CIRCUS

Barbara Cox

PICHARD & DROUHIN

Copyright © Barbara Cox 2009
all rights reserved
ISBN 978-0-9564687-0-3

The right of Barbara Cox to be identified as the author
of this work has been asserted by her in accordance
with the Copyright, Designs and Patents Act 1988

Published by Pichard & Drouhin, London
www.picharddrouhin.com

Contents

1. Cats Only 1
2. New Arrivals 5
3. The Show 16
4. On the Road 27
5. At the Farm 43
6. Part of the Circus 48
7. Ping and Maria 55
8. Accidents 70
9. Benjamin's Story 78
10. Back in the Woods 87
11. Marmalade 95
12. The Cats of Mau 104
13. Well-Fed Slaves 109
14. The Circus Comes to Town 116
15. Celebration 125

Illustrations

Benjamin in the shopping bag .... *frontispiece*
"Buster found two cats" 37
"A new sensation on the high wire" 69
Listening to the story 106

1. CATS ONLY

Out at night in the country, away from the streetlights, the roads were dark and silent.

The birds were asleep, apart from the owl which drifted hungrily over the fields. Other hunters - a pair of foxes and some rats - slipped quietly through the grass ... and then stopped and stood still in astonishment.

Something very strange was coming down the road. Or rather, a procession of very strange things.

The female fox, or vixen, thought they were like cars, but much smaller. They were odd shapes, and some of them seemed to be held together with string. They had engines, which sounded, thought a rat, quite like lawn-mowers. There were nine of them. And from all of them there wafted on the air to keen noses the scent of ... *CAT.*

The field mice had dived out of sight almost before they'd realised what they were smelling. The rats slipped away into the grass, swaggering a little to show how unafraid they were. The foxes sat down in the middle of the road and stared.

The strange vehicles came towards them, their engines chugging quietly. The first one, which looked quite like a caravan, was driven by a lean tabby cat with a torn ear. In the passenger seat was a skinny black cat with both ears intact but a nasty scar over one eye. The tabby slowed the caravan, and leaned out of the window.

"Yeah?" he asked. "What you looking at?"

"Never seen cats in a tin before," answered the dog-fox rudely. The vixen giggled.

The other vehicles were slowing down and stopping. Cat voices could be heard quietly from further back. "What's the problem?" "Couple of foxes in the way." Cats were slipping quietly down from the cabs of the vehicles. "Shall I wake Buster up?" "No, we can handle it."

Suddenly the foxes found that ten very tough mean-looking cats were walking softly and purposefully down the road towards them.

"*Oh*," said the dog-fox, "oh, right, you want to drive through *this* way? Sorry, mate, I didn't realise. " He stood up and sauntered to the side of the road, the vixen hastily following.

"We ought to be getting over to the hen-coop anyway," she said. "You know what it's like," she added to the nearest cats with a nervous smile, "leave it too late and there's nothing left."

Slightly disappointed, the tough cats turned and made their way back to their vehicles.

The foxes were still inquisitive. "What is this, then?" the dog-fox asked. "Some kind of travelling fair?"

"It's the Kochka Circus."

"Circus? Trapezes and that? Not trying to be funny but you don't look like entertainers to me, " said the dog-fox.

"They're all asleep," said the skinny black cat, getting back into his cab. "We're the hunter-drivers."

"Oh, right."

"Can we come and see the show?" asked the vixen.

"Sorry, madam, cats only I'm afraid," the tabby cat

leaned down and released some kind of hand-brake.

The vehicles trundled past and away. The foxes watched them go.

"That's a bit exclusive, isn't it, cats only?" said the vixen.

"Typical," said the dog-fox, pouncing on a slightly deaf shrew which had missed the whole thing.

He immediately forgot all about the cat circus, but a few times that night the vixen wondered about it. She wondered if there were custard pies; she had heard of them but never quite understood what they were.

Just before dawn the odd collection of vehicles arrived at their destination, which was the edge of a small wood near a town. Other vans were already parked there, and other tough-looking, weather-beaten cats had just finished putting up a big tent.

Swiftly the drivers parked the trucks with the others, forming a neat semi-circle around the tent. The tent and the trucks were in brown and green colours, and everything was skilfully placed under overhanging branches of big trees; a passing human would never notice there was anything there which had not been there the day before. They might perhaps vaguely think they had glimpsed some old boxes.

"Where's young Rip with the refreshments?" asked the black cat as he finished putting up an awning from the side of the first caravan.

"Over there somewhere. Oi, Rip!" shouted the torn-eared tabby.

"Sh-sh," said the black cat with a warning glance at the caravan. But nobody stirred inside.

"It's all right, she sleeps like a kitten. Not like her Dad."

"He used to drive you crazy. Couldn't get any work done. Ah, there you are, Rip, you young tiger, where were you? "

A young cat had appeared, his mouth full of a bunch of freshly-killed mice held neatly by their tails.

"Horry," he said through the tails, "houldn't harry em all at wan."

He dropped the mice down on the ground and the black cat, whose name was Sam, scooped one up with his front paw, threw it in the air, caught it in his mouth and ate it in three swift munches.

"Aah," he said. "That's better."

The tabby, who was known as Ted the Ear, was already on his second.

"Nice bit of mouse, that," he said. "Hits the spot."

Sam peered out from under the trees. "What do they call this place, anyway?"

"Dunno," said Ted. "Wales, I think."

2. NEW ARRIVALS

As Miss Kate Kochka woke up, stretched - black and white, slim and elegant - and jumped off her bed, she heard voices raised outside.

She pushed her caravan door open and looked out.

Outside, Sam and Ted the Ear were staring down at a small bundle which was being firmly held under the paw of another of the hunting cats, a big female called Martha.

"He'd had a mouse and half by the time I caught him, cheeky beggar."

"What d'you think this is, a free restaurant?"

Miss Kate walked towards them and could see that the bundle was a small and unattractive young cat. He was a dark brown tabby, and even though his colouring concealed much of the dirt, he was noticeably grubby.

"Stealing food?" she asked.

The three hunters turned respectfully.

"I just caught him, Miss Kate," said Martha. "Right inside the food tent."

The small cat was squashed to the ground under Martha's enormous paw. "Let him up," said Miss Kate, thinking the creature looked more like a bat than a cat with its thin pointed face under huge ears. "Where have you come from? How did you get in here?"

"Through the woods, I came through the woods."

"Check the security, Ted, or they'll all be in."

"Right away," said Ted the Ear, and hurried off. Miss Kate, Martha and Sam stared severely at the small cat.

"I want to join the circus."

"What?"

"I want to join the circus," said the small cat again.

"Do you indeed. And stealing our food would be the right way to start, would it?"

"Please, I was very hungry. And there was such a lot."

"And can you do anything useful? Are you an acrobat or a clown or a juggler? Can you fly through the air or escape from tight corners?"

"No, not really. But I could learn, I could try, I'm not very good at heights though."

The little cat was so humble that Miss Kate began to feel quite sorry for him. Usually the runaways who turned up were conceited young tomcats, and they quickly got bored with all the hard work and went back home.

"Have you been a pet? Have you run away from a house? Because the last thing we want is fifteen humans tramping all over the place looking for Tiddles."

"No. I was living in the woods with Mam - with my mother - and then she got run over."

"What's your name?"

"Benjamin Mew."

"Well, Benjamin," said Miss Kate, "you can go along with Sam and Martha and have a proper breakfast, and then they can see if there are any odd jobs for you to do. If you're useful, you can stay. If not, or if you steal anything else, you'll have to look for another career."

"Thank you miss. Thank you very much."

She nodded to the two hunters, and turned away.

New Arrivals

Rip was standing nearby, waiting to speak to her. "What would you like for your breakfast, Miss Kate? There's sausage this morning."

"Sausage? How very pleasant..."

Sam and Martha headed for the food tent, Benjamin trotting nervously between them. Sam looked down at him. "That was Miss Kate Kochka. She's the boss around here, so whatever she says, you do it."

"Is that why it's called the Kochka Circus?"

"That was her Dad, Thomas Kochka. He set it up, or maybe his father before him, I don't know. He retired - what, couple of years ago now?"

"Must be all of that," said Martha. "She's better to work for than he was, more fair, but she can be a bit sarcastic."

They had arrived at the food tent, where mice, rats, sausages and sardines were laid out on low tables and the circus cats were helping themselves.

"This food doesn't get here by magic," said Sam. "So you be grateful. The hunting team on duty have put in a lot of hard work to get all this."

"Specially the sausages," said a nearby hunter with a grin. "Butcher threw a broom at us."

"So us working cats, we all eat here. The artistes - that's the performers - they mostly fetch the food back to their caravans." Martha gulped down half a rat and took a drink of water from the bowl in the middle of the table.

"D'you have this much food every morning?" Benjamin still couldn't believe his eyes.

Sam and Martha laughed. "Morning *and* evening. And snacks in between."

"Oh, *please* let me stay."

"You can hunt a bit, then, can you?" asked Sam. "If

you've been living in the woods, what d'you get, little mice, voles? Baby birds?"

"I'm not very good at mice," said Benjamin. "I'm better at beetles, really."

"Beetles? No wonder you're thin. If you want to join the circus we'll have to build you up a bit."

Benjamin hadn't in fact particularly wanted to join the circus; he had particularly wanted a square meal. It had seemed a good thing to say to the big cats, to get them to let him stay around long enough to eat something. But now he sat in the food tent, nibbling a bit of everything and then going back to nibble a bit more, drinking clean water, discovering the tastes of sardine and sausage, and watching the circus cats with wide eyes.

The circus cats were tough, but he could tell they wouldn't be stupidly cruel like some other cats he'd met. And they were so sure of themselves, so unafraid. Benjamin was tired of hiding from other cats, avoiding dogs and foxes and badgers and big rats and humans and even owls. He wanted to feel safe. He was beginning to think it would be very good to belong here.

By the evening, Benjamin had had a wash and several good meals and was already looking fatter. He had helped Sam and Ted take some ropes and lighting equipment into the main tent. He walked quietly around the encampment, anxious not to annoy anyone, looking for other ways to make himself useful.

The circus cats were preparing for the night's show, which would be at two o'clock in the morning by a human's clock. Most of the artistes were in the main tent, practising and warming up, evening being their main rehearsal time.

Miss Kate was sitting outside her caravan in the last of the summer sunshine, doing some accounts using an abacus, which as you probably know is an ancient kind of calculator: cats tend to use them because can easily be worked with paws and need no batteries. Miss Kate muttered to herself as she clicked the abacus beads along their different rows.

"Twenty-five and seventy-one, ninety-six... and two hundred and fifty-one is - "

"Three hundred and forty-seven," said Benjamin without thinking.

"What?" Miss Kate clicked rapidly. "Yes, it is. You're very quick, aren't you?"

Benjamin looked scared, as usual. "Sorry. I'm just good with numbers."

"So, divide that by twenty-eight, then."

"Twelve point three nine two."

"Two decimal places'll do, thanks. Come and sit up here."

Benjamin jumped up onto the bench next to Miss Kate and wrapped his skinny tail nervously over his paws.

"Add that lot up. I'll race you."

Benjamin looked at the numbers, and just knew. He always did. "Seven hundred and eighty-three."

Miss Kate clicked the beads across as fast as she could, but it still took her a good minute longer. "So it is."

She looked sharply at Benjamin with her clever green eyes. "Where did you learn to do that?"

"Please, I've always been able really, but Mam taught me as well. She said it ran in the family."

Benjamin always looked especially miserable when

Cat Circus

he mentioned his mother. Miss Kate looked at him for a moment, but she didn't ask any more questions.

"Good," she said briskly. "Now we know what your job's going to be. You can be my Accounts Assistant."

Benjamin seeemed to grow an inch taller and his whiskers stopped drooping.

"Sit there and finish that lot. I've got a meeting in a moment - in fact, here they are now."

Two cats were coming across the grass towards them. One was a middle-aged male tabby. Benjamin stared at the other one. She was young, pale grey, and long-haired, with an amazing tail ending in a plume of darker grey. The golden late sun caught her fur and made it glow. He had never seen such a pretty cat in his life.

The grey cat caught his admiring stare and looked away. Benjamin thought it was a bit snooty of her.

Miss Kate went forward to greet them.

"Tonton, what a pleasure to see you again."

"Miss Kate." The tabby cat, Tonton, touched noses. "Always so elegant. This is my niece, Maria Louisa Grisette."

"Angélique's daughter? ...Your mother was one of the best acrobats I've ever seen."

They went into Miss Kate's caravan. She left the door open, and the windows were open too: Benjamin could hear their conversation.

"Do sit down," Miss Kate said. "I was sorry to hear Papa Minou passed away, but of course he was a good age. One of the old school. It's a shame his circus is closing."

Tonton replied: "It seems he owed money that no-one knew about. So everything has had to be sold."

"Ah, well. So, Maria, are you an acrobat too?" There was a slight pause, and Benjamin could imagine Miss

New Arrivals

Kate staring at the pretty Maria with her clever green eyes.

"I - " Maria began, but Tonton interrupted. "She prefers the high wire. I've been training her, she's coming along very well."

"I've been the high wire act with the Minou Circus for nearly a year now," said Maria. Her voice came out too loud, she sounded nervous. And a bit conceited, thought Benjamin.

There was another little silence.

"We have a high wire act already," Miss Kate said coolly. "Tonton, your message said you were looking for work for both of you. Of course I can always use a cat of your talent, with such a fine career behind you, but I don't think I've got anything for your niece."

Tonton answered quite calmly. "She's a bright young cat, and she looks good in the ring."

"Mm," said Miss Kate. Again she left a little silence. Then she said: "This is a bigger circus than the Minou, my dear, you'd just have to fit in with everyone else and do what needs doing. You can't expect to be a star here."

Maria didn't answer for a moment; when she did, she sounded unconvincing. "That would be all right, I know I need more experience."

Benjamin smiled a little as his paws flipped the abacus beads. *Sounds to me like she absolutely does expect to be a star,* he thought.

Miss Kate said: "All right then, let's see how it goes."

"We're most grateful," Benjamin heard Tonton say. "We'll join right away if you don't mind."

Sam and Ted the Ear came up to the caravan. Sam had a harness on with various tools hanging from it.

"What's this then, doing sums?" asked Sam.

"I'm going to be the Accounts Assistant." Benjamin

tried to sound cool about it, but failed.

Sam and Ted laughed. "Thought she wouldn't let you sit around for long," said Ted. "Is she in there?"

"There's cats visiting."

"Oh, right, we'll wait then."

Benjamin felt proud as the two older cats sat down beside him and he swiftly finished the figures. He was the Accounts Assistant. It was hard to believe that the woods where he had been so miserable were still only just over there, a matter of yards away. He could see the gap in the hedge where he had sneaked through.

"Time she had a new caravan, really," said Ted, noticing the rust marks on a bottom panel. "This is a bit of a heap."

"Why are all the trucks and vans so funny?" asked Benjamin.

Sam and Ted pretended to take offence.

"What a thing to say."

"Funny? What d'you mean, funny?"

"Well, they're all made out of bits."

"So are all cat vehicles. You ever seen one that was different? We make 'em up out of what we can get hold of, don't we? Lawnmowers, abandoned cars, wheelbarrows, you name it. Creative engineering, that's what it is."

"We are cats, you know. We can't call up a car showroom and order a new Mercedes."

"I used to know a cat -" Benjamin stopped.

"What about him?"

"Nothing."

Maria and Tonton came out of the caravan, jumping swiftly down the steps, and walked away.

"Pretty cat," said Ted.

"Don't she know it, though," said Sam.

New Arrivals

"She's not happy about something," said Benjamin.

And indeed, they could see Maria and Tonton were arguing fiercely as they walked away across the grass.

"So," said Sam, "Accounts Assistant, what's your name, Benjamin. Where're you going to sleep, then, if you're staying?"

"I don't know."

"Can't sleep in the truck every night. You and Martha got any room, Ted?"

Ted rubbed his torn ear. "Not any more, we're storing a load of stuff for the Russians."

"We're packed like sardines in our van. Have to ask the boss."

Miss Kate appeared out of her caravan. "You can get on with this window now, Sam. Have you finished those figures, Benjamin?"

"Yes, Miss Kate."

"We were thinking about somewhere for him to stay." Sam and Ted went into the caravan and reappeared at the window.

"Yes," Miss Kate said thoughtfully. " The clowns have got room but I'm afraid they'd be a bad influence."

Ted grinned as he held the window catch for Sam to lever out a bent nail.

Benjamin sat quiet. Miss Kate skimmed through the finished accounts. "Very good. Put them up in the caravan for me, and the abacus, just put them on the table... Well, perhaps I'll ask Buster if he could make room for you."

Ted and Sam made faces through the window to Benjamin which suggested this would be a very good thing.

"And see the show tonight, Benjamin," Miss Kate continued. "You need to know what we're all doing here." She walked off towards the main tent, waving her elegant

Cat Circus

black tail.

Benjamin collected the accounts and took them up into Miss Kate's tidy van.

"Well, you're honoured," said Sam, hammering a new nail into the window catch.

"Who is Buster?"

"He's the star of the show," Sam said. "The Magnificent Buster, Strongest Cat in the World. Amazing, the stuff he can do. D'you remember, Ted, when he did the routine with the chains, breaking free?"

"Unbelievable. And he's a nice fellow, too, good company. Haven't you seen him around?"

"Is he very big and orange?"

"That's him. You've landed on your feet and no mistake."

As Benjamin went out again to collect the abacus, he glanced over at the woods.

Then he quickly glanced again. No, there was nobody there. For a moment he had had the feeling someone was there, watching him. But there was no one to be seen.

The Magnificent Buster, a giant of a ginger cat, was putting some equipment away after his evening practice when Benjamin walked timidly towards him.

"Please -" he began, but Buster interrupted him cheerfully.

"Ah, you're my new lodger. Bob, is it?"

"Ben. Benjamin."

"Come on inside, then, Ben."

Inside the caravan Buster seemed bigger than ever. He was a really huge cat. But the caravan was big too, and

New Arrivals

very comfortable. Buster showed Benjamin the bed he could use, and a shelf for his things. Benjamin said he didn't have any things, but Buster grinned and said it was amazing what one picked up, travelling around. He was so easy and ordinary to talk to that Benjamin quickly forgot he was a famous star.

"So, living in the woods, then, eh?" Buster said. "Must have been a bit miserable."

"It was all right at first. But then they - my mother got run over."

"Did she not know to mind the traffic?"

"Some cats were chasing her and she ran out under a car," said Benjamin sadly.

Buster looked at him for a moment, but like Miss Kate earlier, he didn't ask any more questions.

"Right," he said, easing his enormous orange self onto his wide bed. "I'm going to have a sleep now before the show tonight. Come and go as you please, you won't wake me up."

He curled up, wrapped his huge tail over his big pink nose and was asleep in an instant.

Benjamin jumped up onto his own bed. *This is my own bed,* he thought. *Well, it's borrowed, but it's a bed and it's mine to use.* There had been a bed, before the woods, but he didn't want to think about that. *I can come and go as I please.* He stretched, washed his right front paw, and then tucked both his front paws in as he sat neatly like a tea-cosy, purring. *And tonight I shall see the show.*

3. THE SHOW

A small neat cat Benjamin hadn't seen before showed him to a seat, saying "You should be all right here, but if it gets very full I'll have to ask you to stand."

Benjamin was going to say that was fine, but the neat little cat had already moved away.

It was a quarter to two in the morning, the human world was mostly fast asleep, but the cat circus was buzzing with anticipation. Seats in the big tent were already filling up fast, cats in ones and twos and big family groups, kittens chattering excitedly, parents busy keeping them in order.

Benjamin had never seen a circus before, but most of the cats sitting near him seemed to be very familiar with it all. He could hear them saying things like "I've heard these Burmese are amazing" and "Oh, but there's nobody to match Buster. He always gives you such a great show."

The small neat cat showed a very fat family to the seats in front of Benjamin. The mother had a large bag which was twitching.

"Can I remind you," said the small cat sternly, "that in the interests of safety all live refreshments must be consumed before the performance begins."

"No problem," said the father, "just a snack." The mother reached into the bag and brought out a live mouse

The Show

for each of her kittens. They chomped on them noisily; the youngest dropped the tail of his mouse and dived onto the floor to look for it.

The traditional cat instruments were already in place on the bandstand: drums of different sizes, tubular bells, cymbals, tambourines and a zither. Now the musicians came in and took up their places.

The audience hushed expectantly. There was a tremendous roll on the biggest drum. A voice from nowhere announced: "Miss Kate Kochka proudly presents the legendary KOCHKA CIRCUS!"

Another drum roll drowned the applause - then suddenly something black and white raced past Benjamin's right ear - another black and white form leaped down the opposite aisle - and a black cat with white paws jumped from high up in the tent and landed in the middle of the ring. The clowns had arrived! All the kittens in the audience cheered.

Benjamin knew that the two black-and-white clowns were the brothers, Mog and Mig, so the other one must be Maggi. They all seemed to be quite mad. To the sound of frantic music they chased their tails, did backwards somersaults, pursued each other round the ring and bounced in and out of the audience, tickling kittens, stealing food, pulling the tails of respectable fathers of families, sitting in the laps of elderly females. Benjamin couldn't believe what they got away with.

Then as quickly as they had appeared, they were gone, the music changed, and two fluffy golden Persian cats, Zorrat and Zarin, stalked into the ring and began to juggle, their fur waving like cornfields as they flipped brightly coloured fake-fur mice into the air with their big deft paws. The musicians kept up a soft hypnotic music behind them. At last they had a completely unbelievable number of mice - even Benjamin couldn't count how many - flying through the air above and between them, and they coolly, calmly kept the flow up as if it was nothing at all while their big paws moved so fast they were just a blur. The audience gasped in amazement.

A young cat brought on a top hat and set it down in the middle of the ring, and the two Persian cats calmly flipped the mice into it until it was full to overflowing and they had just one left each. They balanced these on their little short noses and then nose-juggled them backwards and forwards from one to the other. Everyone cheered. Still impassive, the Persians collected the last two mice, bowed, barely acknowledged the applause, and trotted out of the ring, their big golden tails waving.

Quick as lightning the clowns were back, imitating the Persians' distant manner, trying to juggle and failing, getting kittens to join in. Mog and Mig picked up a tiny kitten from the front row and juggled with it, causing its mother some alarm.

There was a drum roll, then another. The tiny kitten was popped safely back in its seat, looking a bit dazed, and then the whole audience burst into applause as the Skakatovs ran into the ring.

The Russians. Benjamin had already heard the way everybody in the Circus just said "the Russians". There were eight of them in the ring altogether, and he had no idea which was which. They all had sleek short silvery grey fur and slanting green eyes. Some of them were grown up, some were young cats about Benjamin's age, and there was one who was hardly more than a kitten.

Swiftly they pushed a seesaw and a platform into position in the middle of the ring, and then the two heaviest

The Show

grown-up ones jumped down from the platform onto one end of the seesaw, propelling a younger one off the other end and into the air. Each time as they went up into the air the young ones turned somersaults, twisted, flew over each other's heads and did other amazing things, each more daring than the last. It seemed as if the whole ring was full of flying, leaping silver bodies and waving tails, while the musicians were playing a wild Russian-sounding tune.

Now the younger Russians were flying up to land on each other's backs and form a pyramid of grey cats, three at the bottom, then two, then one, then the smallest one on the very top. The two big grown-ups were watching warily in case anyone should fall.

The young Russians leaped down and stood ready - the musicians went mad with drum rolls and wild chords on the zither - and Buster sauntered into the ring. All the cats in the audience cheered.

Buster took a quick bow, then strolled to the front of the ring. He stood sideways to the seesaw. The musicians were silent, but a drummer was poised by the biggest drum...

Womp! The drummer hit the big drum hard with his front paws and as it boomed, a Russian cat flipped up from the seesaw, somersaulted and landed on Buster's back. Womp! Another one, two somersaults. Womp! A third one, a somersault with a twist. Now three Russian cats were standing in a row on Buster's back. Womp! Another one landed on top of them. Womp! Another. Wrrrrromp! The second youngest of the Russians was now standing on top. The silver pyramid of cats had re-formed, but this time supported on the huge ginger back.

The smallest Russian was poised ready on the seesaw.

Wrrrrr - the big Russians jumped down - the little one flew up - rrrromp!! He landed at the very top of the pyramid, stood up on his hind legs and waved to the crowd.

The fat young cats in front of Benjamin were bouncing up and down in their seats. The applause was deafening.

The Russians jumped down and trotted round the ring in an elegant silver stream, while Buster stood calmly in the middle. Then he walked off, leaving them to take another bow, and then the unseen voice announced that there would be an interval of twenty minutes.

Everyone streamed out into the dark summer night, chattering and laughing.

The small neat cat stood at the entrance. "Enjoying it?" he asked as Benjamin went past.

"It's brilliant."

Benjamin went with the crowd, dazzled with the excitement and the skill of the performers, hardly noticing the cats around him -

- then he stopped, froze.

Over by the entrance, Sam, Ted, Martha and a couple more hunter-drivers were talking to two cats who were trying to get in. It didn't look like a friendly conversation.

The cats just in front of Benjamin noticed them too. "Argument over there. Maybe somebody tried to get in without paying," said one of them, without any great interest. "Look, there's sardines," said another and the group headed away across the grass.

Benjamin walked along beside them, so the cats at the entrance couldn't see him. Then as they reached the sardine-seller, he ducked down, slipped between two caravans and doubled back along the line of vans until he could hear what was going on at the entrance. He felt cold and sick.

"Look, mate," Ted was saying, "we've told you, we don't take in runaways and strays. The boss don't like it, and anyway they're no use."

"This is a circus, not a doss-house," Martha said. "We're professionals, we're trained for what we do. We don't let just anybody wander in."

"But you're obviously very busy cats," said one of the strangers. "All we're saying is, this young scallywag could have slipped in and hidden somewhere without any of you knowing."

His voice was pleasant and persuasive, but Sam was not impressed. "If that was possible, we'd have every kitten in the neighbourhood sneaking in and watching the show for free."

"We have excellent security, believe me," said Ted.

The other stranger, a female, had a smooth, chilly voice of someone used to giving orders. At the sound of it, Benjamin's fur stood on end. "You see - and you must forgive us for insisting - this young cat is really very disturbed. He would cause all sorts of mischief. As you say, you're professional cats, and I know some of the circus acts are dangerous. This young one is the sort who would damage equipment, you know, just for the fun of it. He does need to be with cats who can manage him, who understand his problems. It really would help set our minds at rest if we could search the circus."

"That's out of the question. There's a performance going on."

"Oh, we can wait till afterwards. But we won't be happy until we've searched, d'you see?"

"What seems to be the problem?" Miss Kate's crisp tones broke in.

"Looking for a runaway, Miss Kate," said Sam. "We've told 'em we've nobody here, but they're not inclined to believe us."

"Are you the owner?" The male stranger sounded friendly, but a little impatient. "We need to find this young cat, he's quite a danger to himself and other cats. He's thin, small for his age, a dark tabby colour, big ears. We think he's hiding in your circus, but your staff here aren't keen to allow us to search."

"Nor am I. We're only here for one show, we've a lot to do tonight. And why should we allow strangers to rummage through our homes and belongings?"

"I can assure you," said the female," that if this young cat is in your circus, you'll regret it."

"Will I, indeed?"

"I mean, you'll regret it because he's a troublemaker. He causes mischief and bad luck wherever he goes."

"And how long exactly have you been looking for him? We only arrived here last night."

The male stranger paused for a moment before he said: "We've been looking for him for a while. But I passed by the circus this afternoon and I thought I saw him."

"Small, dark, thin... I think the cat you saw would have been Jeffrey Leftpaw, the front-of-house manager. He's a very dark tabby."

"But -"

Miss Kate interrupted. "I think we've made ourselves clear. We're harbouring no runaways, our security is second to none, no-one comes into the circus that I don't know about. We are not going to allow you to search any part of the circus. You may stand here by the entrance as the audience leaves, and check that your lost cat is not among them. That's all I can do for you, Madam and Sir. We leave here tomorrow so I don't expect we shall meet again. Good-night."

Staring through under the van, Benjamin saw Miss Kate's neat paws walking away. He heard the female cat hiss briefly.

"We don't need that sort of language," said Martha.

Keeping as flat to the ground as he possibly could, Benjamin slunk back along the row of vans.

Reaching Buster's van, he slid under it and then waited for a group of cats to pass by, going back to the tent. As they passed, he darted up the steps and pushed the door open.

"There you are, young Ben," said Buster. "Enjoying the show?"

"Yes, but some cats are after me. I have to hide."

"Ah, right," said Buster. "Pop in there, then." He opened a small cupboard at floor level, pulled out an embroidered blanket which was inside. Benjamin went in; there was just about room for him and the blanket, which Buster tucked back in between him and the world.

"There you are, you'll be safe there. Don't worry. Shame, though, you'll miss the second half. I think I'm going to be rather good tonight."

From his hiding place, Benjamin could hear the music and applause coming from the tent, and then the happy chatter of the audience going past the caravan on their way home.

Then everything went quiet.

It seemed like a very long time before he heard the

door open and soft cat footsteps. For a second he cowered in terror, but then he heard Buster's voice: "Come in, sit down. I'll get the little chap out."

The door of the cupboard opened and Buster pulled the blanket away. Benjamin emerged, blinking.

Miss Kate, Ted the Ear, Sam and Martha were all in the caravan as well as Buster. There was hardly room for them all.

"Come right inside, please, Sam, make sure the door's closed," said Miss Kate. Buster jumped up onto his bed, leaving space for Sam to come inside; the self-closing door swung shut behind him.

Benjamin stood in the middle, looking smaller and more bat-like than ever, surrounded by these big, strong, determined cats.

"Have they gone?" he asked.

"As far as we can tell, yes. They're nowhere to be seen around the circus," said Miss Kate.

Martha added," But they may be up in the woods somewhere."

The cold that had swept over Benjamin when he first saw the two cats was still there. Fear was back. It had never really gone.

"Thank you for not giving me away," he said. "Why didn't you?"

"Didn't like the look of them," said Ted the Ear.

"Specially not that female," said Martha.

"So you know them, don't you?" Miss Kate's penetrating green eyes were fixed on Benjamin. "A female all white with one tabby paw, a male ginger-and-white, both very pleasant, very polite, on the surface at least. "

"Yes. I know them."

"Sam, Ted and Martha all felt they were not to be

trusted. So did I. On the other paw, we all felt you could be trusted. You should repay us now by telling us what's going on."

Benjamin felt a bit wobbly. He sat down on the floor. "My Mam used to work for a very bad cat. She hated it and we left. But he didn't want her to leave because she knew things about what he was doing. So he sent those two - Jack and Tabbyfoot - he sent them after us." He was trying to keep his voice steady. "They followed us a long way. Then we thought we were safe in the woods. But they found us. They chased Mam onto the road, they did it on purpose and she died. And now they're after me..."

It was all too much. Benjamin crouched down and began to howl, which is the cat version of crying. Gulping, howly miaows came out of his mouth and his ears were flat against his head. Buster stretched down a huge paw and patted him awkwardly on the back.

Miss Kate waited till he calmed down a bit. "We're leaving here tonight. We don't usually travel after a show, but we've got a long way to go. We'll be on the road for three days. D'you think they'll bother to follow us?"

"I don't know."

Buster said, "It depends if they really think he's with us, or they just came round on the off chance."

"They were pretty keen to search the circus," said Sam. "I think they reckon he's here."

Miss Kate thought for a bit. "Let's see what happens," she said. "Ben, you keep out of sight until you're told otherwise. That means you don't leave this caravan. I'll get Jeffrey to be out and about as much as possible - he is the same sort of colour as you, though I have to say his ears are much smaller. But perhaps, if they follow us and they're watching, they might believe he was the one they saw."

"Thank you." Benjamin sniffed.

"We're acting on our instincts, and believing you and not them. But we could be wrong. You could be stringing us along here, playing games with us, and they could be telling the truth. If anything happens to make it look as if you haven't been straight with us, we'll have to reconsider. You understand?"

"Yes, Miss Kate."

"Right, then. Sam, Ted, Martha - let's get the show on the road."

The three hunter-drivers pushed the door open and briskly left the caravan.

Miss Kate paused for a moment, looked down at Benjamin and then at Buster. Buster shrugged. Miss Kate nodded.

"We shall see what we shall see," she said, and left, with a wave of her black tail. The door swung shut behind her.

Benjamin felt completely exhausted. He gave another little howl.

"Ah well," said Buster. "You know what they say, it's a great life if you don't weaken. Jump up on your bed, young Ben, might as well be comfortable. Could you manage a bit of pilchard? There should still be some in the dish."

4. ON THE ROAD

The caravans moved through the night. Buster, curled up in a huge orange mound on his bed, was fast asleep and snoring quietly.

Benjamin was not sleeping. He sat wide awake, his ears nervously pricked. He had never been in a moving vehicle before and it was taking a bit of getting used to. Also, he was terrified that Jack and Tabbyfoot would find some way to stop the caravan and get him out.

He felt like a coward. *You're sitting in a caravan with the strongest cat in the world,* he said crossly to himself, *and you're still frightened?* But he knew it wasn't stupid to feel like this. Jack and Tabbyfoot were clever and ruthless. He didn't believe they wanted to capture him, he believed they wanted him dead; and they could find plenty of ways to do it.

He was upset at the way they had tried to turn his new circus friends against him. Though recent events in his life had made him timid, Benjamin was shrewd: he knew that Miss Kate and the hunters would remember the things that were said about him, even if they didn't believe them now. As soon as anything went wrong, they would start to wonder about him. Miss Kate had said as much. Then they would stop protecting him.

The caravan slowed and then stopped. Benjamin

sat there, tense. He thought he heard movement from the driver's seat, on the other side of the partition. Then nothing happened.

After a while Buster opened his eyes a little.

"What's happening?" Benjamin asked nervously.

"No problem. We always stop every few hours, have a snack. If you want a pee, now's your chance."

"I'm all right, thanks."

There was a scratch at the door. Instantly, Buster was wide awake - he threw a big squashy cushion on top of Benjamin, hiding him.

"Come in," he said.

In came the young hunting cat Rip with a mouthful of mice which he dropped on the table. "Just fresh caught, Mister Buster, that do you?"

"Great stuff," said Buster.

As soon as Rip left, he uncovered Benjamin again and threw him a mouse.

"Did you get any sleep?" he asked

"Not really," Benjamin said. "I expect I seem like a real little wimp to you, but I can't stop thinking about those cats."

"No shame in that - after what happened to your mother, I'm not surprised they're on your mind." Buster crunched up a couple of mice with alarming speed. " You are little, though. Have another mouse." He watched Benjamin as he ate. "You'll grow to a good size, you know, you've got big paws."

"And ears," said Benjamin with his mouth full.

"I was too polite to mention the ears. But you'll grow to them. Poor diet's obviously been your problem."

The mice had all disappeared. Buster wiped his face quickly with a huge paw.

On the Road

"Shan't be a moment," he said. "Nature calls." He shouldered the door open and then turned for a moment to add: "If anyone comes to the door, hide."

Without his huge bulk, the caravan seemed big and empty. Benjamin sat there, wishing they had travelled a thousand miles away from Jack and Tabbyfoot. He also wished he could sleep.

After what seemed like a long time, Buster came back in.

"I've had a word with the Russians," he said. "They said you can ride with them for a bit, later. You'll like them, they're a cheerful lot. Better company than me, I need a lot of sleep, you see."

He settled back on his bed as the caravan started moving again. "Yes, diet's definitely been your problem. A regular supply of fresh mouse, you won't know yourself. When I was your age, I was four times your size."

"Were you with the circus then?"

"No, I'm from a farm family. We ate well. Rat, mouse, milk fresh from the cow, baby rabbit in season... we were all big, my Dad was a big cat, but I grew up the biggest, so I thought I'd make a living out of it."

"My granny and grandpa were farm cats. I didn't know them, but Mam said."

"Ah. It's a good life, but, well, one rat's much like another once you've caught a few hundred of them. The circus, there's always something interesting going on." He yawned, exposing massive fangs and a vast expanse of pink mouth. "But I do sleep a lot, have to rest the muscles. Don't worry, small Ben. We'll keep you safe."

And Buster was fast asleep again, his huge tail wrapped over his nose.

Benjamin did feel reassured, and his stomach full of

mouse was calming. He curled up, and began to feel his eyes closing...

He woke up to find the caravan had stopped again, and Buster was standing in front of him, holding a shopping bag.

"Hop in here," said Buster. "I'll take you on a visit to the Russians."

He held the bag open and Benjamin got in. Cautiously Buster opened the door and looked out, then swiftly he jumped down to the ground, carrying the bag, and made his way along the row of caravans.

Benjamin couldn't see anything from inside the bag, though he could tell it was still dark. He felt them go up the steps to another van, and heard Buster scratch at a door.

"Only me," Buster's voice said. They went into the van.

Buster let the door close behind them and then tipped Benjamin out onto the floor. He landed upside down and heard a lot of cats laughing.

He picked himself up, feeling stupid. He looked around.

All but one of the Russian cats he'd seen in the circus ring were there, plus another grown-up female and a kitten. With Buster as well, there was hardly room to move in the van. But everyone was smiling at him in a friendly way.

"He's got BIG EARS," said the kitten.

"Sorry," said a young female of about Benjamin's age. "My sister is very very spoiled and rude."

"Well, he has," said the kitten defiantly.

"Tasha, enough," said an older cat who was

obviously Tasha's mother.

Buster said: "These are the Skakatov family. This is Benjamin. He doesn't know anything about the circus, so you'll have to explain things to him. I'll come back for you at the next stop, Ben. Have a good time. Get Olga to tell you some stories, she knows good ones."

He took the shopping bag and ducked back out of the van. When he'd gone, there was quite a bit more space.

"Now then," said one of the older females. "I'm Vera." Vera was the cat Benjamin had not seen in the ring; she was rather plump. "My husband Dimitri is driving the van. These are all our children - Igor, Irina, Rudi and Vladimir." Vladimir was the little one who had waved from the top of the cat pyramid.

"And I'm Sasha," the grown-up male said. "I'm Dimitri's brother. This is my wife Olga, and you've just heard from our daughters Tonya and Tasha. Now d'you know who everyone is?"

"Not really," said Benjamin, feeling stupid.

The Russians laughed. "No one ever does," said Sasha. "We don't mind."

The caravan started moving again. Olga made room for Benjamin on the bed where she was sitting with Tonya next to her and Tasha the kitten cuddled up in her lap.

The Russians relaxed. Most of them were purring and the soft sound filled the van. Benjamin felt almost safe.

"Did you see our act?" asked little Vladimir.

"I only saw the first half of the show," Benjamin said.

"We do some more in the second half, but you saw the pyramid then, it's good, isn't it? I'm the one at the top."

"Yes, I saw you. It was very good."

"You dug your claws in my back again, Vlad," said Tonya, "I wish you wouldn't do that."

"Mama," said Tasha.

"What?"

"Mama, why do cats purr?"

"It makes the world go round," said Olga. "If we didn't purr, the world would stop spinning and then where would we be?"

"Stuck," said Vladimir.

The van jolted a little as it travelled along a rougher patch of road.

"Mama, why does the world go round?"

"Because it does. That's what worlds do."

"Are there other worlds?" Tasha looked puzzled.

"Of course there are, you've seen them," said Tonya. "Up in the sky, look - "

She went towards the window, but Sasha said quickly, "Tonya. Leave the curtains closed."

Tonya came back and sat down again.

"Why are there worlds?"

Tonya sighed and looked at Benjamin. Her baby sister got on her nerves.

"Who put them there?"

"Well," said Olga. "Someone. We don't know who Someone is. It's not for us to know. But we know that our world belongs to Cat Goddess."

The older cats, including Benjamin, had all asked the same questions as Tasha was asking and had all been given this answer by their mothers. But it was good to hear it again. They listened with a comfortable feeling.

Olga said, "Cat Goddess made all the different lands and seas, and then she made all the different kinds of cats. She made the tigers, the lions and the cheetahs, the jaguars and the ocelots, the cougars, the leopards, the lynx, and the Mau which are our own ancestors. Then she made all the other animals, for cats to hunt and play with; when she first made them, they were the right size to be prey - everything, cows, gorillas, humans, elephants, they were small so that we could hunt them, play with them and eat them when we chose. "

Tasha was listening wide-eyed. "Really small?"

"Yes. Mouse-sized, rabbit-sized. But something happened. Some say the Rat God was jealous of Cat Goddess's beautiful world, some say that Someone has an enemy who tries to undo what Someone has arranged. Anyway, many of the other animals found a way to get bigger. The Rat God or the Enemy Being gave them a spell to say or a drug to take - all this is long ago, and we don't know what happened. But they got bigger, and began to take over the power in the world. Humans are the worst, of course, because they're quite clever too. So now these creatures are unnaturally large, and we are at a disadvantage. The jaguars have retreated into the forest and the cougars to the hills. And humans hunt everything, even the tigers and lions."

"Will they win?" Tasha looked worried.

"The lions are lazy," said Olga. "They might let power slip away. But the tigers will never be defeated. And we believe that this wrong state of things will not last for ever, and that one day the prey will all go back to its right size and the world will be as it should be."

"And we can have elephants for tea," said Vladimir.

The cats fell silent apart from their purring, thinking their own thoughts. Benjamin was remembering his mother sitting under the oldest oak tree in the woods, telling him about the other animals getting to be the wrong size, and how he had wished the badgers would be small again because they frightened him with their big stripey faces and huge claws.

"What are you going to do in the circus?" Rudi, who was also about Benjamin's age, asked him quietly.

"Nothing like what you do. I'm hopeless at jumping and I'm scared of heights. But I'm good with numbers and Miss Kate says I can be her Accounts Assistant."

"You'll be very useful," said Tonya. "We're all the other way round, we can turn somersaults but we can't add up."

"Mm. I do want to stay."

"Let's hope it all works out for you," said Olga quietly.

Again he woke as the caravan slowed down. He felt rested, at last. And he did need a pee.

Around him the Russians were stretching their elegant silver limbs. Benjamin turned to Tonya as she woke up, and whispered: "I need to go outside."

"Mama," said Tonya more loudly than he would have wished, "Benjamin wants a wee. It's all right, Ben," she grinned, " we'll all come out and stand round you."

Benjamin was embarrassed, but he was learning that in this big family everyone teased each other.

Sasha went to the door and looked out. "I think it's all right, slip out quickly and go under the van. Be careful, though, it's nearly light now."

But just as Benjamin finished filling in the hole he'd dug under the van, suddenly the air was rent with the wild screeches of a terrible catfight.

There were yells, screams and growls from several cats, and he heard other cats running towards the sounds. He saw the paws of some of them flash past the van.

"Benjamin!" Sasha said urgently, peering under the van. "Back inside, quick!"

Benjamin dashed up the steps into the Russians' caravan.

"What is it?" he asked, panting.

"Sounds like it's in Buster's van. All the hunters have gone there now. No, stay here, Rudi, this is serious."

The Russians were all trying to see out of the van, squashing into the doorway, but Benjamin didn't need telling to stay out of sight. The sounds of the fight rose to an insane crescendo, many voices now, and then the sound of running paws dashed past the van - first one cat, then several in pursuit.

"Who was that, running away?" Igor, the oldest son, asked his uncle as they peered out of the door.

"Don't know," Sasha said. " Never seen her before." He looked back at Benjamin. "White cat with a tabby paw, mean anything to you?"

"Yes."

"Uh-huh."

Now it was quiet outside.

"Sounds like the excitement's all over," said Vera, the plump mother cat. "Ah, there you are, dear."

The other Russians stood back from the door to let Dimitri in. He was the biggest and strongest of the Russians, and looking annoyed.

"Whatever next?" he said. "Buster went for a walk to stretch his legs and came back to find two cats going through his caravan. Cheek!"

"Is he all right?" Benjamin asked.

"Buster? Of course he is. Sounds like he'd done some damage to both of them before the hunters got there. One of them got away though, Martha and some of the boys are after her but I think she's got clear. Honestly. Can't even park up your caravan in peace, I don't know what the world's coming to."

This is what I've brought with me, Benjamin thought.

"Excuse me," a young female voice was raised outside. "Could someone tell me what on earth's going on?"

Benjamin realised it was the pretty young long-haired cat. Maria, that was it. Maria Louisa something.

"There was a fight," Sasha, who was still by the door, said to her politely. "It's all been sorted out now."

"Does that sort of thing happen often in this circus?"

"Never happened before since I've been here."

"I'm glad to hear it."

Maria obviously went away. Sasha looked back at the others.

"Someone woke the princess," he said.

"Was that that new cat?" asked Irina. "She is such a little madam."

"She's a looker, though, " said Igor, Irina's elder brother.
"You'd fancy anything, you," said his cousin Tonya, and got a quick tap across the ear in return. "Don't be cheeky," Igor said. Tonya shook her ears; she didn't seem bothered.

"She is pretty," said Benjamin.

"Ah," said Igor. "Spotted her already, have you? Mystery cat. I can see we'll have to watch you with the ladies."

Buster appeared in the doorway, blood trickling from a nasty scratch on his forehead, carrying the shopping bag.

Olga and Vera both said "Are you all right?" at the same time.

On the Road

"Buster found two cats going through his caravan"

"I'm fine. It was all a bit unpleasant, but we should be moving off again soon."

"The other one got away, then?" asked Sasha.

"Looks like it. Martha's just come back."

Sasha nodded and went out to take his turn driving the van.

Buster held the shopping bag for Benjamin. "Do we need that now?" Vera asked. "Can't be too careful," Buster said. "Somebody must have told them something, why else did they head for my van?"

"Come back soon, Benjamin," said Olga.

"Yes, any time," said Vera.

"Come and teach me how to do sums," said Tonya with a grin.

Benjamin got into the bag.

Safely back in Buster's van, he was astonished at the mess when Buster tipped him out onto what had been his bed.

"Yes, it did get a bit violent in here. But there's something I want you to see before we go. I didn't mention it in front of the kittens."

Buster led Benjamin to the door and opened it a crack. Benjamin peered out, and gasped.

Lying at the bottom of the steps was a bloody mess of ginger and white fur that had once been a cat called Jack.

"Thought you might want to see that," said Buster. "Because of your mother and all."

The caravan suddenly started moving and Benjamin fell back from the door. He had one more glimpse of his dead enemy as the door swung open and then shut.

"Mind," said Buster," we've got to be even more careful about you being seen."

"She got away, then, Tabbyfoot."

"Yes." Buster licked his right front paw and wiped the blood away from his scratch. He seemed to be otherwise unharmed.

Benjamin had to ask. "Was it you that killed him?"

"We all piled in. He was a good fighter, I'll give him that. But the thing is, they must have a spy in the circus. Why else did they think you were in here?"

Benjamin sat silent for a moment. *Jack's dead.* He had a memory of Jack and Tabbyfoot chasing his mother and - he shook his head to clear the picture away. He felt strained and anxious. Nowhere was safe, after all. "I can't stay, can I? I'm bringing all this trouble."

"What are you talking about? None of us is hurt - Ted nearly lost his other ear but he was never much to look at anyway. Maybe a few sensitive artistes had their beauty sleep spoiled." Buster had obviously heard the pretty Maria complaining.

Benjamin seemed unconvinced.

Buster looked him firmly in the eye. "Listen to me, Ben. When we want you to go, we'll tell you. All right?"

"Yes. Thank you."

"Just keep out of sight and take it easy. Not too easy though, the reason I got you back here is so you can help me clear up this van."

The circus moved on through the early morning countryside. As they sorted out the mess, Buster told Benjamin about the other circus artistes.

"I thought you'd like the Russians, everybody does, they're a good lot. The Burmese are a nice family too, the Naga Family they're called. They do the trapeze, they're probably the best in the world right now. But they're very intense, they practise and train all the time, so you don't see much of them. The clowns are idiots, don't have anything to do with them."

"They seemed insane," said Benjamin.

"They are. I mean, you've got to have clowns, the kittens love them, and at least these don't do any of that sad clown stuff which really gets on my nerves. But I suppose you could say they're practising all the time too - basically they're the same off stage as on."

"I saw the jugglers. They were very good."

"Zorrat and Zarin. They're tremendous jugglers, the best. Be careful what you say to them though, they're cousins and they can't stand each other. Anything you say always seems to get taken the wrong way and end up offending one of them."

"Why do they perform together if they don't get on?"

"Oh, they're from a circus family," said Buster, picking a cushion up off the floor and discovering a large tear in it. "A lot of them don't get the choice, you know, they're in the family act as soon as they can walk - look at young Vladimir. And I expect they'll soon have little Tasha up in that pyramid too. Somebody'll have to lose some weight though, or my back won't stand it. I was glad when Vera decided to retire from the act, I can tell you. Lovely cat, but she is well covered." He put the cushion to one side. "I'll see if I can get someone to mend that. Who else is there you haven't seen? Oh, yes, Mademoiselle Ping, the tightrope walker - high wire, we call it. Charming cat, but very shy. You won't see much of her."

"That new cat Maria wants to do the high wire."

"Does she indeed? She'll have to wait her turn. Now her uncle, Tonton, he used to be in a famous trapeze

On the Road

act. I remember seeing him when I first started. And I think her mother was an acrobat. I seem to remember she left the business and went to live with some pet cat who had rich humans."

The caravan was back to normal. "That looks better," said Benjamin, jumping up onto his bed.

Almost at once, the van stopped again. Buster lifted a corner of the curtain and peeped out.

"That's good. We've covered a bit of distance before it's got too light. What with all the fuss and palaver holding us up, I thought we might get behind schedule."

"I suppose I'd still better stay in here."

"I'm afraid so. We'll be parked here all day, move on as soon as it gets dark. We're heading right out into the country so we can get a lot of distance covered."

"Will there be a show tonight?"

"No, not for a while now. This is just a stopover, and in a couple of days we'll be at a farm where we always rest up for a bit. It's a good place, let's hope you'll be able to come out and explore it."

"Where will the next show be?"

"Something for you to remember," said Buster. "In the circus, you never talk about where the next pitches, the stops, are. A rival circus or a fair might have a spy, you see, and when they found out where you were going then they'd go to the places first and take all the audience. Queering your pitch, it's called."

"I see. But you know everybody in this circus, don't you? You can trust them all?"

"Yes, and no. You never quite know. Cats have their own reasons for doing things. At the moment I certainly don't trust everyone. Now then, young Benjamin, before breakfast, let's see you lift these ten times."

Cat Circus

Buster plonked two small weights down on the floor. Benjamin looked at them. They had loops to fit his paws into.

He put his paws in and lifted. "Oof," he said.

"Good," said Buster. "And again. One, two, three, lift, that's the way to do it. One, two, three, keep going... A few weeks with me, you won't know yourself."

5. AT THE FARM

The deserted farm was on top of a hill, surrounded by meadows where cows grazed quietly, flicking their tails to keep away the flies in the hot summer sun.

No people had lived at the farm for a long time. The house was locked up, and an owl was living in the attic. The barn was used sometimes by the cattle for shelter, if the weather suddenly turned bad in the autumn or spring; the sheds and outhouses had mostly fallen down. It must have once been a much grander place - there was a round brick dovecote, and even a little ruined chapel - but the rusting tractors had been left there by a farmer now long forgotten, and there was nobody to recall its history.

The circus cats had tucked their vans in between the dovecote and the back of the barn, well out of sight. Most of them were outside in the sunshine, resting, chatting, enjoying the break in their journey.

The Russians were lolling about, arguing with each other in their cheerful way, apart from Vladimir who was chasing his tail. The two Persian jugglers were grooming their long fur, the same colour as the cornfield in the distance; for once, they seemed to be on good terms with each other. Miss Kate and the little neat cat Jeffrey were sitting chatting on the steps of her caravan. Mademoiselle Ping the tightrope walker, a slim Siamese, was lying by herself gazing dreamily out across the fields. At the other end of the barn, the clowns were trying to push each other into a patch of nettles. A short distance away, the hunter-drivers were playing a game of five-a-side football with very few rules.

Buster was stretched out in the sun in front of his caravan, seeming to take up yards of space. He appeared to be asleep, but his eyes were not quite closed, and he was keeping a watchful eye on everybody.

Inside Buster's caravan, Benjamin sat on his own, feeling increasingly like a parcel.

He'd been in the caravan for three days now. What was the point in being with the circus if he had to hide away for ever? And how long would it last? How long before the circus cats decided he was too much trouble? In spite of what Buster had said, he had his doubts.

Still, if I'd stayed in the woods I'd be dead by now. At least this way I may end up a few jumps ahead of Tabbyfoot and whoever else she gets to help her out - there's plenty she can choose from.

Outside, Buster stretched, yawned, got up and idly wandered back into his caravan.

"It's pretty quiet out there," he said. "I reckon you could at least pop into the barn. The Nagas'll be practising, you can watch them for a bit if you like."

"That would be good," said Benjamin.

"Where did I put that useful length of rope?" said Buster as he got the shopping bag out.

When the circus was at the farm a couple of years before, the Nagas had climbed up in the roof of the barn and fixed up some ropes to hang down from the high

At the Farm

beams. They liked to know that they would be able to get some practice in whenever they stopped here.

There were four in the Burmese family, two couples: Kchown and his wife La, Nay and his wife Kalay. They were probably the best cat trapeze act in the world, and they knew it - but knowing it just made them even more dedicated to staying the best.

They were swinging and climbing up and down the ropes with amazing ease as Buster strolled in, carrying his shopping bag which seemed to be full of another length of rope. The Burmese called cheerful greetings to him, but didn't stop.

"I didn't know if you wanted this other piece of rope," said Buster loudly.

"Thanks," they called down. "Maybe in a moment."

Buster sat down in a pile of old and rather mouldy straw and put the bag down beside him.

"Sorry, Ben," he muttered. "You'll have to stay in the bag. Some other cats here."

Benjamin peered through the coils of rope but couldn't see anything. Then he heard a voice - or rather a furious whisper - and recognised it as Maria's, coming from the other side of the heap of straw.

"I was just getting known," she was muttering. "Now everybody'll forget about me... I'll be just nothing, handing other cats their props and turning a couple of cartwheels, I was doing that years ago. I wish things could be like they used to be."

Benjamin heard Maria's uncle Tonton sigh. "That's the business we're in. You take the work you can find. Get used to it, Maria."

"Papa Minou -"

"Papa Minou used to spoil you rotten. Now things

Cat Circus

are different. If all you want to do is whine, go outside, cats are working here."

"All right then. I'll go and practise walking round the ring, shall I?"

The pretty Maria crossed Benjamin's line of vision, swishing her beautiful tail, stalking out of the barn.

"Wants it all handed to her on a plate," said Tonton's voice, obviously to Buster. "Her mother was exactly the same."

"She'll learn," said Buster. He moved the bag round so Benjamin could look up and see the four Nagas as they swung the ropes backwards and forwards and jumped from one to the other in mid-air.

Back in Buster's caravan, Benjamin said: "I'm not sure I can go on like this."

"Yes," said Buster, " I do realise a shopping bag is no place for a young cat, but that's just why it's a good thing to use. I'm sorry I couldn't let you out in the barn, but I don't know Tonton very well. I'm sure he's all right, but you can't be too careful."

"But, you see, it's all very well being careful, but it's driving me mad."

"You're a lot braver with a few good meals inside you," said Buster, but not unkindly.

"I know. I owe everybody here such a lot and I want to stay with the circus. But I'm just hiding all the time, I don't see any point to it."

"Those cats that came after you were very nasty pieces of work."

"I know that," said Benjamin bitterly.

"Of course you do," said Buster. "But the fact is, if

At the Farm

they'd caught you we wouldn't be having this discussion."

"You saved me and I'm really grateful. It's amazing the way you've all protected me, when you don't know me at all really. But if this is the way it's going to be, I'd rather take my chance on my own again. Anyway, I'm just bringing trouble to the circus. They could have hurt you."

"They weren't that good," said Buster.

Benjamin suppressed a smile. He was getting very fond of Buster. And the big orange cat was right - he was feeling braver since he was well rested and fed. But it wasn't just that: he still felt powerless.

"The thing is," he said, "when I was in the woods I was a hunted animal. I was always waiting for them to turn up. And I thought if I joined the circus, I could feel different. But of course, I'm still being hunted. So it doesn't help."

"Well, give it a chance. We're moving away from them all the time. If we can be sure we've left this Tabbyfoot behind, then you can start a proper new life."

They tracked us down before, thought Benjamin. *She's not so easy to leave behind.*

"I know it's tedious," Buster said. "But one way or another things'll change, they always do. "

6. PART OF THE CIRCUS

Tabbyfoot didn't re-appear, and obviously Buster and Miss Kate had a few discussions that Benjamin didn't know about, because once the circus left the farm and arrived at its next pitch, they began to let him have more freedom.

On the night of the second performance, Jeffrey, the small neat front-of-house manager, came to find him in Buster's caravan and said: "You could see the second half tonight if you like, you missed it before, didn't you? Come round at the interval, you can stand at the back where you won't be seen."

So Benjamin saw the Russians in their second act, in which they swung on a huge swing which catapulted them up into the air, and again they flipped and somersaulted and made themselves into a silver-grey cat pyramid without any apparent effort.

The clowns looned about again; they had a routine involving a clockwork artificial mouse, almost as big as themselves, which whizzed around the ring almost as madly as they did.

The Nagas were every bit as breathtaking as everyone had said: for the first time he understood why it was called the flying trapeze. They seemed to have nothing to do with the laws of gravity.

Part of the Circus

The only act that left Benjamin a bit cold was Mademoiselle Ping, the tightrope walker. Perhaps the slender Siamese wasn't as good at showing off to the audience as some of the others. She did difficult things and did them well, but there was a bit of excitement missing somewhere. When she took her bow, Benjamin suddenly caught sight of Maria, sitting in the back row. She was watching Mademoiselle Ping with an expression that clearly said : *I could do better than that.*

Finally, the closing act, into the ring walked Buster. At least half the audience cheered, including Benjamin. And his act was tremendous: he lifted weights (painted to look like enormous tins of cat food), standing on one paw sometimes, then balancing on a see-saw. He carried huge chains on his back. He invited kittens from the audience to come and be lifted up, and then adults too.

One tough tomcat, who obviously wanted to prove Buster couldn't do it, looked very surprised when he found himself suddenly lifted high in the air above the ginger cat's huge head. For his closing turn, Buster lifted a big wicker basket containing all the younger Russians and the three clowns - a task made harder by the fact that the clowns didn't keep still for a moment.

Buster had his own confident, good-humoured way of presenting every amazing feat - he would show the audience what he was about to do - show them how impossible it was - and then do it, in a way that said: *Impossible, huh?* The Nagas and the Russians were superb performers, but there was no doubt Buster was the star of the show.

After the performance, Benjamin slipped quietly back to the caravan. He had a quick look round as the happy crowd wandered off towards the exit, but he couldn't see anyone suspicious.

Soon Buster came in, and Benjamin knew him well enough by now to know what to say. "I thought you were absolutely brilliantly fantastic," he said. "The most incredible thing I've ever seen."

"Yes, I thought it was one of my better nights," said Buster. "Have you eaten all those sardines?"

So the circus moved on through the summer countryside, a show here, two shows there, the odd vehicles moving off in groups from one site as the warm darkness fell and arriving at the next in the freshness of dawn as the big tent was being put up in its new place.

No strange cats appeared, nothing strange or worrying happened. Gradually Benjamin allowed himself to believe that Tabbyfoot had lost their trail, or given up. And over the next few weeks, he became a normal member of the circus and ate, worked, chatted and relaxed with the other circus cats.

He found the accounts he had to do for Miss Kate were easy, and he quickly had them up to date, tidy and clear to understand. Miss Kate was pleased and relieved, it was a job she had always hated.

Jeffrey, who was extremely precise by nature, had long discussions with Benjamin about what exactly was the best way to record the takings each night. Benjamin couldn't care less, as the numbers all added themselves up for him anyway, but he liked Jeffrey - and even more, he liked the feeling of being part, even if a junior part, of the management of the circus.

The Russians were becoming his good friends, especially Tonya and Rudi. But everyone was friendly to

Part of the Circus

him. He was accepted, and it was a good feeling. Buster was like a kind, easy-going uncle, and he realised what the big cat had done for him by agreeing to take him into his caravan. "Everyone's nice to me," he said, " because I have the Buster seal of approval."

Buster liked this idea. "Ah," he said, "but I wouldn't have approved you if you didn't deserve it."

Benjamin noticed that though the circus cats seemed to have rapidly decided he was all right, they had equally rapidly decided they did not like Maria Louisa Grisette. The pretty young cat was really unpopular. She was usually referred to as "The Princess" or "Little Miss Attitude" and remarks like "Honestly, would it kill her to say thank you?" were frequently heard.

She was now the cat who carried the top hat in for the jugglers, and they seemed to be the only ones who got on with her - but then, they were too busy arguing with each other to bother about anyone else's manner. She also had to do some simple acrobatics with a couple of young cats, to fill in while equipment was being put up, and this seemed to be what she really hated.

The two young cats were Ted the Ear's kittens and wanted to be hunters when they grew up, but still they thought their little act was a good laugh and always did their best to entertain; but Maria had a way of making them look clumsy in the ring, which certainly didn't go unnoticed by the senior members of the circus.

One evening, Benjamin and Buster were strolling back from the Russians' caravan and passing by Mademoiselle Ping's van when they heard a little muffled howl from inside.

Buster went up the steps and pushed the door open. Benjamin heard the little howly noise again.

"Ping, old kitten, what's the matter?"

Ping just made sniffling sounds.

"Have a drink. Have something to eat," said Buster. "Benjamin, pop over to the food tent and pick up some of those pilchards for Ping. And a drop of milk if they've got it."

When Benjamin came back with the pilchards and milk in a dish, Mademoiselle Ping was explaining to Buster.

"Every evening when I practise, she sits in the tent and stares at me."

Benjamin put the food down on the table without saying anything. He guessed she was talking about Maria.

"Thanks, Ben. There you are, Ping, look, get stuck into that."

"Oh, I can't eat all that, I have such trouble keeping my weight down."

"Nonsense," said Buster. "You're distressed, you need to build up your nerves. Anyway, if you can't finish it, Benjamin here'll have some. He's got to grow to fit those ears."

Ping managed a weak smile, and nibbled a bit of pilchard.

"So what form does this staring take, then, that it's upset you so much?"

"She's trying to put me off. I'm sure she wants me to fall and hurt myself. And when I make a mistake, she laughs."

"Does she now?"

Ping calmed down after a while, and they left her to herself. Outside her van, Buster said: "Would you find Tonton for me, and ask him if I could have a word when he can spare the time?"

Benjamin found Tonton easily - he was always in

Part of the Circus

the ring practising with the Nagas. He passed on the message politely, but none of the circus cats would dare keep Buster waiting, and Tonton came straight over to the caravan.

"Your niece," said Buster without any introduction, "needs sorting out."

Briefly he explained what Ping had said.

"Excuse me asking this," said Tonton politely, "you don't think Mademoiselle Ping is exaggerating at all?"

"I've never seen her upset like that," said Buster. "She's highly strung but she doesn't make things up."

"Thank you for speaking to me about this," said Tonton, looking grim.

He went out of the caravan at once.

And Maria was right outside the door. "There you are, Tonton, I didn't know where you'd gone to."

Buster and Benjamin could hear his furious reply: "I've been hearing complaints about your behaviour. Again. What is your problem, Maria?"

Tonton was obviously so cross he didn't care who heard - or maybe he knew that being told off in public would be the worst punishment for his niece. Certainly anyone in the nearby vans would hear him.

"I hate it here," Maria was saying, "they're all horrible, I didn't want to come here in the first place."

"Listen to yourself," said Tonton. "What are you, a kitten? This is the nicest bunch of cats I've worked with in a long time. Just because they don't spoil you –"

Maria began to howl. "They hate me! I hate them! I don't want to stay here!"

"Rubbish. I've never heard such nonsense. You've made no effort to fit in."

"I'm going to run away," sobbed Maria.

"And do what? Where would you live? What would you eat? You've never caught a mouse in your life."

"I'll go and live with humans."

"Oh, well, if *that's* what you want," said Tonton with complete contempt. "We'll drop you off at the next cat refuge. I'm sure they'll be queuing up to take you home and have you as their ickle puddy wuddy."

Maria howled, a bit more quietly.

"And all this with Mademoiselle Ping, what on earth are you up to?"

"She dyes her fur," said Maria.

"Really, I hadn't noticed."

"I think she's a white cat really and she dyes herself to look Siamese. How stupid," said Maria. "Who ever heard of a Siamese with green eyes?"

"Ping's appearance is none of your business. You should be making friends with her, getting her to teach you things, not behaving like some jealous amateur."

" What would she teach me? She's rubbish. I'm better on the high wire than shee-*eeoww!!*"

Benjamin was watching out of the window, he looked back at Buster. "He smacked her round the ear with his claws out! It must have really hurt."

"I'm ashamed of you," Tonton said, and walked away. Maria looked around for somewhere to hide, but there was nowhere. She trailed along behind Tonton towards their van.

"Poor thing, she's so embarrassed," said Benjamin.

"Deary me," said Buster.

7. PING AND MARIA

Everyone in the circus heard Maria had got a telling-off, and most of them said "About time too." The row was the main topic of conversation the next day: most of the cats thought Tonton had gone too far by hitting Maria, but the general view was that she'd asked for it.

She kept out of sight for most of the day. But at about five in the afternoon, when Benjamin was sitting on a bench outside the caravan eating a snack, he was surprised to see her walking towards him.

She jumped up onto the bench and sat down without saying hello. Benjamin looked at her sideways as he finished a piece of sausage.

"So," said Maria. "How did you do it?"

"Sorry?"

"You just turned up here out of nowhere and everyone thinks you're terrific. How did you do it?"

In spite of her rude manner this was obviously a serious question.

"I don't know," said Benjamin, "I've wondered myself. I think perhaps it's because I don't look like much and I can't do anything."

"You can, you're brilliant at the accounts, everyone says so."

"Yes, but none of them want to do that. I mean, I

can't do anything circusy."

"So you're no competition."

"Mm. But if you meant why do they like me and not you, I don't think you're unpopular just because you're talented and you look good." Benjamin said this as a statement, not a compliment, and she took it the same way.

"Why then?"

"Well, because they all love this circus and it's so obvious you don't want to be here."

"No, I don't," said Maria. "She didn't want to take me on, Miss Kate. She only wanted my uncle. I'm just an extra. And I was a star, before. I know it was only a little circus and we didn't travel very much, but I was quite famous, cats would recognise me and all that, and I loved it."

"I think they do understand that here. They just reckon you're, well, pretty arrogant really."

"And they're not? Some of them act like they own the world. They ought to understand that I have talent too."

"Look, I don't know about all this artistic temperament stuff. But we're both the new arrivals. I can tell you this is a whole lot better than where I was before. You feel like it's worse than where *you* were before. But we're both here. We have to fit in."

Maria sighed. "I suppose so."

The circus was quiet - all the other cats were either rehearsing or having a nap or a bite to eat in their caravans. Maria and Benjamin sat there for a little while in silence. Then, to their surprise, Mademoiselle Ping came out of her caravan and walked over to join them.

"Hello," she said. "I just wanted to say to Maria: I'm sorry I got you into trouble."

Ping and Maria

Maria stared at her. So did Benjamin. *I wouldn't have said that,* he thought. *That's really nice of her.*

He got down from the bench. "Would you like a seat?" he said.

"Thank you," said Mademoiselle Ping and jumped up to sit next to Maria.

Benjamin sat on the caravan steps just nearby. He felt it was really only Maria that Ping wanted to talk to.

"Hurts, doesn't it?" said Ping. "I always hated getting hit on the ear."

"Tonton has never ever ever hit me before," said Maria.

"Oh. I used to get hit all the time."

Benjamin and Maria looked at her, surprised. Ping was older than they were, old enough to be their mother, in fact; close up, she looked tired.

"Were you very naughty, then?" Maria asked.

"Oh no," Ping said. "It was the high wire. I didn't want to do it, you see, I was frightened. But if I complained, I got hit."

Maria was having the unusual experience of forgetting all about herself, as she stared at the older cat. "You didn't *want* to do it?"

"No, but my father decided. It was all his idea, how I look and everything. I had to do it, we needed someone in the family to be working and he'd got ill and couldn't perform any more."

Maria was silent for a moment as she took this in. "But you're grown up now, you don't have to do what other cats want."

Ping smiled bitterly. "I still have to work. And this is all I know how to do."

Benjamin could see that Maria felt quite different

about Ping now. "I'm sorry I was a nuisance while you were practising. It's just that I *do* love the high wire, you see."

"You should have asked to practise with me. I wouldn't have minded."

Maria hesitated. "Is it too late for me to ask now?"

"I don't know," said Ping. "You might try and push me off the wire."

"I wouldn't do that!" said Maria. Benjamin thought Ping was joking, but if so, Maria didn't get it and the older cat gave no sign either way.

"Start tomorrow evening," she said, and jumped down and returned to her van.

Maria sat quite still, watching Mademoiselle Ping until the door closed behind her.

Then she leaped down onto the grass, turned three somersaults and a cartwheel, and then bounced up to Benjamin and kissed him.

"That'll be quite enough of that," said Benjamin.

Somewhat to Benjamin's embarrassment, Maria now decided he was her friend.

She would dash up to him after her practice with Mademoiselle Ping, and chatter away about problems of tight-rope walking which meant nothing to him at all.

"You see, she does the balance on the front paw before she does the back flip, but I find if I do that, I'm positioned wrong for the next movement, but I don't do a back flip then anyway, because Tonton and I worked out some much more interesting things to do - "

"Don't tell Ping that, you'll upset her again."

"Of course I won't, silly, she's my friend now. But I

have to say - " Maria lowered her voice and looked around before she went on: " - she's really skilled, but it is a bit dull, her act, don't you think?"

"I wouldn't know," said Benjamin, who did know what she meant but didn't trust her not to tell the world anything he said.

"There's something else about her that I can't quite work out," said Maria, still quietly. "Sometimes, especially at the beginning of practice, she's very sort of slow, and she even loses her balance."

"Really?" Benjamin was surprised. "From what she said, she doesn't enjoy doing it much. Maybe she just has to get in the mood."

"Mm." Maria sighed. "How can she *not* enjoy it? "

"Not everyone wants to wander about on a bit of string miles up off the ground."

"It's not string, stupid. And it's not all that far up, it's wonderful when you're up there."

"I'll take your word for it," said Benjamin.

Maria started talking about her own act, which she was now being allowed to work on with Tonton, though only at odd times when the ring was free.

Benjamin had seen her practise one part of the act, where she made circles and patterns with long ribbons of different colours, holding them in different paws as she changed position on the wire. It looked very pretty, and he did think it was better than what Mademoiselle Ping did, but he didn't say so, Maria being quite conceited enough already in his view.

Maria's favourite routine, which they were still developing, needed a fine invisible wire strung across above the high wire, from which hung several big silk butterflies; Tonton would work this wire so that the butterflies danced above Maria's head, and she would jump and somersault on the high wire as she tried to catch them.

"You see, the idea is that it just looks like I'm playing and doing whatever comes into my head. But it needs a lot of work to make it look like that."

Benjamin and Maria were sitting on the steps of Buster's caravan. Tonya and Rudi came past on their way to the food tent.

"Learning all about the circus, Ben?" asked Tonya.

"Nothing like expert tuition," said Rudi.

Most of the circus cats thought Maria was nicer lately, but the Russians were obviously never going to see her as anything but an annoying little know-all. Benjamin was trying to stay on good terms with everybody, which wasn't always easy.

Maria ignored their sarcasm, but waited till they'd gone before she said: "Would you come and watch me practise sometimes, Ben? It really helps to have an audience, even if -"

" - even if it's only me?"

"Um, well, yes. You know what I mean."

"I know exactly what you mean. He doesn't know anything so he'll be easy to impress."

"I *didn't* mean *that!*" Maria said in outraged tones, before she realised he was teasing. "Oh, shut up," she said.

A few days later, he wandered into the big tent when he knew Maria would be there.

The tent was quiet, the rows of seats and the ring itself were empty, clean and ready for the night's audience. Maria was with Ping, up on the wire.

There was no one else around: the safety net was in

Ping and Maria

place so they didn't need anyone to stand by in case of accident. Maria had explained to him in great detail that cats perform on the trapeze and high wire without a safety net or harness, but for practising they always have a net so they can try things out and not worry about falling. "Naturally we'd land on our feet, but we could still be hurt or even killed by a bad fall."

Benjamin sat down quietly and watched.

Ping and Maria were working practising back somersaults on the wire. They each did several, with what seemed to Benjamin like a ridiculous amount of skill.

Suddenly something extraordinary happened. Ping went quite still for a moment, wobbled, and fell off the wire. She dropped like a stone down into the safety net below, and just lay there.

Benjamin jumped out of his seat and ran down to the edge of the ring.

Maria leaped down off the wire into the net. It bounced like a trampoline as she landed and she scrambled over to Ping.

"I'm all right," said Ping, faintly.

"No, you're not," said Maria. "What happened?"

Ping pulled herself together a bit and licked a front paw.

"Well?" said Maria. "Don't tell me you just slipped."

Benjamin stood at the edge of the ring; he could see into the middle of the net where they both were. There was a long moment while Ping looked at Maria, then she lifted her head a bit and looked round to see if anyone else was there. She saw Benjamin.

Then she said, "You both have to promise not to tell anybody."

"Of course," said Benjamin.

"Not anybody, not even Tonton." Ping looked intensely at Maria.

"All right," said Maria.

"I have this thing wrong with me. All my joints hurt me, especially in my legs. Sometimes it hurts so much I don't know what I'm doing. But I've never blacked out like that before."

"Have you seen anybody about it?" Maria asked.

"I know what it is. My father had it, that's why he had to give up his career. If I tell anybody, they'll make me retire and then I don't know what I'll do."

Maria sat back in the net and looked at her. "Well, Ping, if you fall off the wire without a net it won't matter what your future career is, 'cause you'll be dead."

"Thanks Maria, that's just what I wanted to hear." Ping said drily; but she got back to her feet and was obviously starting to feel better.

"Come on," said Maria, scrambling to the edge of the net and jumping neatly down, "let's get a sardine and talk about it."

Benjamin and Maria sat in Ping's caravan, Benjamin remembering the time a short while ago when Ping had been so upset by Maria. That was all forgotten now - it was obvious that the older cat was hugely relieved to have someone to confide in.

Maria was trying to persuade her that she must have a safety net for the performances.

"How can I do that? I never have. Everyone would know there was something wrong. Anyway, why do cats want to see the high wire? Because it's dangerous. That's the thrill."

"Couldn't you introduce a new part of the act, and say you have to have the net because it's so risky? Make a thing out of it."

"Miss Kate wouldn't allow it. She'd say if it's not safe enough to do without a net, then I shouldn't do it at all."

They argued about it for some time, but Maria could see that Ping was not going to change her mind.

Benjamin had kept quiet while they were talking about the net. When Maria ran out of steam and the conversation faded into silence, he waited a moment and then said: "Was there something you did want to do? I mean, if you hadn't been made to do the tightrope?"

"High wire," Maria corrected him automatically.

Ping paused before she answered. "I think... I always thought I'd like to be a pet."

Maria stared at her with her mouth half open in amazement. "*Really?*"

"Mm. I know we're free and we run our own lives, but I'd just like to have a house and my meals provided..."

"We have meals provided here."

"As long as we're part of the circus, we do. But what happens to circus cats who can't work any more? Ask Tonton, he's not getting any younger, he must have thought about it."

"He has. He's got cousins who live in France in an olive grove, he's going there when he retires."

"Well, he's lucky," said Mademoiselle Ping in a sour tone.

"But *humans*," said Maria. "Haven't you seen them, they're so *annoying?*"

"It might not be your choice," Benjamin said to her quite sharply. "But there's a lot to be said for being looked after."

"I suppose so, sorry, if it's what you want..."

Ping looked at Benjamin – he was so much more confident now, but he was still the small cat with big ears who'd been living in the woods on beetles. "You know what I'm talking about," she said.

"Yes," said Benjamin. "It's a cold world out there."

When they left Ping's caravan, Benjamin and Maria walked silently towards the van Maria shared with Tonton. They were both thinking the same thing.

"We promised," said Maria finally.

"I know."

"But she's going to have a horrible accident."

"Yes."

"I can be in the ring every night when she does her act. I'm usually there anyway. But I can't catch her if she falls."

They were outside the van, and Tonton had the door open to let in the warm evening air.

"You want some food?" he called out.

"No thanks," said Benjamin.

"We had a sardine with Ping," said Maria. Then she muttered to Benjamin:

"I've got a problem, too, which is if I drop hints or anything, everyone'll just think I'm trying to make trouble for her 'cause I want her job. Which I do, but I'm not *that* mean."

"I could try to let Buster know somehow," Benjamin whispered. "He's fond of Ping. But he'd tell Miss Kate."

"And then Ping would be finished with the circus."

"She'd be alive though."

Ping and Maria

"I keep remembering the way she dropped off the wire. Like a dead cat." Maria shivered.

"What are you shivering for?" called Tonton who could see her through the door. He was wondering what they were whispering about. "It's a lovely warm night. Haven't got the flu, have you?"

Maria and Benjamin exchanged glances. Maria said: "No, but I'm afraid Ping might have. She was a bit out of it this evening."

Clever cat, Maria, thought Benjamin. *We've kept our promise. We haven't told about the illness she's really got.*

"Nice to see you worrying about someone else for a change," said Tonton.

The Russians finished their second routine and ran out of the ring, happy and exhausted, to waves of applause.

Benjamin and Maria were standing just at the entrance to the ring and had to step out of their way.

"Ah, the happy couple," said Tonya.

"Shut up," said Benjamin, his eyes fixed on Mademoiselle Ping who was just going into the ring.

Tonya and Rudi saw that he was in no mood for jokes, and paused beside him, wondering what was going on, as the pieces of the big swing were carried past them.

"Ping wasn't too well today," he murmured to them. "Touch of flu or something."

Maria realised Tonton was standing behind her. He hadn't seemed to take her earlier comment about Ping seriously - but here he was.

Mademoiselle Ping seemed to be all right. She bowed to the audience and began to climb the ladder up to the high wire.

Cat Circus

The drums rolled. The spotlight picked her out, high up in the roof of the circus tent. The audience stared upwards, ears pricked and eyes wide...

Benjamin, Maria, Tonton and the two young Russians all stood in the entrance to the ring, watching.

Ping stepped out onto the high wire. One step, two steps – and froze.

Every performer knows by instinct when this happens to someone else, the thing they most dread and fear – to be in front of the audience and lose your nerve – to have no idea what you are supposed to do next.

Maria knew, in a split second, that it had happened. So did Tonton.

"Get her down!" he said, and ran out into the ring.

Maria followed him. The audience saw them dash across the ring and began to wonder what was happening as Maria started to climb the ladder up to Ping. Tonton stood at the foot of the ladder, tense and ready.

As soon as Maria was near enough she called up, "Ping! It's all right."

Ping still stood on the high wire, not moving a muscle, the lights picking out the colours of her carefully dyed fur, her green eyes tight shut.

Maria reached the small platform at the top of the ladder.

"You don't have to do it," she said. "You don't have to. Life's full of other things you can do. Come on. Step backwards. Come off the wire."

"Can't," said Ping through clenched teeth.

"Come on, Ping. Two steps backwards and you're off."

Far below them was the floor of the circus tent. If Ping fell the way she had last time, she would be seriously injured or killed.

The musicians, uncertain, had stopped playing. The audience was completely silent. Other circus cats had come into the ring - Sasha and Dimitri were standing below Ping, hoping they could catch her if she fell. Every cat in the tent knew something was terribly wrong.

Benjamin was staring up at Maria, trying to put the right words into her mind. *Make her forget the audience, Maria, make her feel like it's just you and her practising.*

And Maria was doing exactly that, making her voice sound as everyday and normal as she could. "Hey, Ping," she said as if they were just going through a new idea, "it's easier if you move your right back paw first."

Ping made no move, but she was listening.

"Right back, then left front, yeah? Just a couple of inches each step. Then left back, then right front. You know, just tiny steps. Try it."

Slowly, slowly, Ping eased her right back paw off the rope and moved it back two inches.

"Yeah, yeah, that's good. That works. Left front?"

Inch by inch, paw by paw, in the total silence of the tent, Maria got Ping to back off the wire, until she could feel the platform beneath her. She flopped down and for the first time opened her eyes and looked at Maria in silent gratitude.

Every cat in the tent stopped holding its breath. There was a small cheer from part of the audience, followed by a buzz of excited chatter.

Tonton was on his way up the ladder. "Come on, I'll help you down."

"Must have been something I ate," said Ping faintly.

"I poisoned the sardine," said Maria and grinned. Ping laughed quietly, but the sound was drowned by a roll

Cat Circus

on the drums, and the voice of Miss Kate.

"Owing to the temporary indisposition of Mademoiselle Ping, we have a change of programme... Tonight and for the first time ever, Kochka Circus proudly presents a new sensation on the high wire, the amazing MARIA LOUISA GRISETTE!!"

Maria's jaw dropped.

"Blimey!" she said. "She doesn't waste much time."

"That's the circus for you," said Tonton. He put two rolls of bright coloured ribbon down on the platform before he carefully gathered Ping up to carry her down the ladder.

Ping looked at Maria over his shoulder. "Go, kitten," she said.

Maria picked up the ribbons: they were hers, the ones she used in her act. They shone as they caught the lights. The audience were waiting.

Maria took a deep breath, flicked her long fluffy tail and ran out onto the high wire....

Accidents

"A new sensation on the high wire"

8. ACCIDENTS

And so things changed, a little.

Mademoiselle Ping decided to stay with the circus for a while and help Jeffrey with the front-of-house management. She let the dye grow out of her fur and quickly became white all over; everyone thought she looked much better, except for Benjamin who had his own reasons for not liking white cats.

Maria was now the happiest feline high-wire artiste in the universe. She was so conspicuously charming and cheerful that several of the circus cats began to wish she would go back to the way she was before.

She no longer had to carry the top hat in for the jugglers: this job had passed on to Lily, who was another one of Ted and Martha's kittens. Lily was quite young and rather nervous, but she was managing all right until one night she picked up the hat and the bottom fell out of it, scattering the coloured mice all over the ring.

The audience laughed, thinking it was a little extra comic touch, but Lily had no idea what to do, and just stood there staring at the mess of mice. Zorrat and Zarin were on their way out of the ring, but they turned swiftly when they heard the laughter, saw what had happened, darted back and scooped up most of the coloured mice, juggling with them as they left the ring. The three clowns came running in and cleverly used the remaining mice in

Accidents

their act. Lily got out of the ring somehow and burst into tears.

Benjamin thought this was all rather funny, though he felt sorry for Lily. He was surprised how seriously everyone took it. Miss Kate interrogated all the younger cats, but none of them had damaged the hat and they were mostly quite insulted to be suspected of it.

"It's a really, really bad thing to do, to touch another artiste's props," Maria explained to him. "I mean, juggling's all right, but most circus acts are dangerous and if someone messes around with your stuff you could get hurt. We all get taught when we're kittens - you don't even pick something up to help a cat who's clearing away their things, not without asking first."

Miss Kate was unable to discover who had damaged the hat. It had been quite cleverly cut, so that the crown of it would stay together until the slight weight of the toy mice made it fall apart. Zorrat and Zarin began to suspect each other, and were soon on even worse terms than usual.

They were now in a busy stage of the tour, with a show every night in different villages and towns. Benjamin was amazed at the number of places where a complete cat circus could park all its caravans, set up a big tent, hunt for food, and entertain the cats of the neighbourhood, without a single human noticing.

No one had much time for socialising, but Tonya and Rudi could always be relied on for a laugh and a joke.

They still loathed Maria, and Benjamin got a bit fed up keeping them apart, but he had come to realise that these likes and dislikes were part of life in the circus. Apart from the squabbling cousins Zarin and Zorrat, the hunter-drivers didn't all get on, though Ted the Ear, Martha and Sam were the undisputed leaders; the clowns were always playing practical jokes on each other which often ended in noisy fights.

Even in the happy Russian family, Igor and Irina considered themselves grown-ups and would get irritated with their younger brothers and sisters - who in turn had a strong objection to being bossed around. The cheeky Vladimir was usually in trouble with somebody.

So when Benjamin noticed that one wheel on Buster's caravan looked distinctly wobbly, he wasn't that surprised that the driver Rip seemed irritated when he mentioned it.

"Looks all right to me," he said.

"Sorry, not trying to tell you your job or anything."

"Should hope not," said Rip drily as he walked away. Benjamin assumed that Rip, who was young and quick-tempered, had had a row with somebody.

But on the road that night, he suddenly woke up as the caravan dropped at one corner with a thud and a scrunching sound, and ground to a halt.

Buster had woken up much faster than Benjamin, he was already on his feet. "Out!" he said, "Straight out now, run and catch up with Miss Kate's wagon, she's just in front."

Benjamin didn't argue. He leaped out of the van, his heart thumping, expecting to see his enemy Tabbyfoot waiting for him. There was nobody, only Rip coming round to look at the wheel which had come completely off its axle. The van behind, which belonged to Ted and Martha, had stopped too, and Ted was getting out to see what was going on.

Miss Kate held her door open and Benjamin jumped

Accidents

up into her slowly moving caravan. A few seconds later, the huge form of Buster jumped in too.

"Bad place to break down," Miss Kate said. "Houses all round. Too many dogs."

Indeed, as they pulled slowly away from the broken-down van, they could hear assorted barking from the rows of dark houses that lined the road.

"I told him that wheel was loose," said Benjamin, and then wondered if he'd said the wrong thing. Miss Kate looked at him very sharply indeed.

"How did you come to notice it?" she asked.

"Rudi was trying to teach me to juggle and I dropped the ball right by the wheel."

Miss Kate nodded, in a way she had which told you nothing at all about what she was thinking.

"My first thought was, it was another trick to try and get hold of young Ben here," Buster said. "But there's no sign of anyone around. And we've left the van behind now. They can ambush it all they like, they'll only get Rip and Ted."

Ever since the fight when Jack had been killed, the circus convoy had frequently changed around the order in which the vans travelled, but Benjamin had noticed that the vans behind and in front of Buster's always had the senior hunters driving them. *Taking no chances,* he thought.

They left the built-up area and travelled through wilder country, open moorland with only a few farms and villages.

For several days they gave no performances, but no one could relax: there were hardly any places for the circus to hide and all the cats felt tense as they travelled through the night across the bare hills and camped for the day behind clumps of gorse and brambles or tucked under huge outcrops of bare rock.

Other odd things happened, too. The rope fastening of the safety net became mysteriously frayed, to the point where it would have broken if a cat had jumped down into the net - luckily Tonton noticed it before the Naga family began their practice session. The signs left at a crossroads by the first vans in the convoy were moved, and the second half of the circus went miles down the wrong road. A batch of sausages, though they were fresh from the butcher's van, gave everyone who ate them a terrible stomach upset.

By the time they came down off the moor and headed into cosy, easy country of woods and fields, all the cats were looking suspiciously at each other.

Miss Kate didn't like it at all. She knew how quickly bad feeling could spread through a small circus community, everyone taking sides and refusing to help each other out, and somehow it always came over to the audience.

It was one thing the jugglers being huffy with each other, that was part of their act, but those little looks and smiles between artistes when a show was going well, that feeling of a wonderful, special, happy world of the circus - that was vital. If you lost that, the show was no longer a treat for the cats who came to see it. They would become critical and easily bored, and the next time the Kochka Circus came round, they wouldn't bother to see it.

She was watching everyone intently, trying to find out the source of the problems. And of course, everyone knew she was watching them, and that didn't help either.

"It's not me," said Benjamin. "I'm sure some of them think it is."

"Why should they?" asked Tonya.

"Well, I haven't been here long."

"Nor have Maria and her uncle," said Rudi.

The three of them were lying at the edge of the circus pitch, which today was behind a disused cowshed down a little lane. It was still hot, though the summer was moving onwards now towards autumn.

Benjamin twitched his ear as a fly tried to settle on it. "But they're circus cats," he said. "You all know where they've come from. I just turned up."

Rudi rolled over in the sun and stretched. "Doesn't matter, they could still be up to something. They could still be trying to sabotage us."

"Nobody seriously thinks it's them. And anyway it might not be anyone, it could all just be coincidence," said Tonya rather sharply. She thought it was bad luck to talk too much about the odd happenings, and she knew it upset Benjamin. "Let's go and look at the sea," she said. "Have you ever seen it, Ben?"

"No, I never have. Is it something special?"

"There's a lot of it," said Rudi. "Come and look."

They walked down the lane between the fields. It was very quiet. Their paws made no sound on the hot stony surface of the lane, and they could hear insects buzzing and a cow chomping grass on the other side of the hedge. High up in the air, a bird sang in a continuous twittering thread of sound.

"Skylark," said Tonya.

"Pretty song. Wonder what they taste like," said Rudi.

Benjamin, as always, was glancing back over his shoulder.

The lane ended, and they took a path going down

the hillside through some woods. Benjamin had noticed an odd smell in the air since they arrived in this place, and now it was getting stronger.

"Here we are, look," said Tonya who was walking ahead.

The other two joined her and looked down through a gap in the trees.

They were above a small bay surrounded by cliffs, with a sandy beach. The waves broke sleepily on the shore, gleaming in the sunshine. Several groups of people with children were swimming and paddling.

"Is that the sea, then?" asked Benjamin. He thought it looked thoroughly unpleasant - cold and wet, and the fact that it was moving about only made it less attractive. "That's where the funny smell comes from."

"Yeah," Rudi said. "Don't ever try to drink it, it tastes revolting."

"The human people seem to like it."

Down on the beach, the children were shouting happily as they played in the waves. Tonya watched them. "Funny, isn't it, the way they like getting into water? Mum says they have it in their houses, they have like a big bowl and they put water in and sit in it and that's how they get clean."

"I suppose not having fur or proper tongues, they're a bit stuck for washing," said Rudi.

"Bath," said Benjamin. "They call it a bath."

Tonya looked at him in surprise. "Did you used to live with humans, then? I thought you sort of grew up in those woods."

"Before that I lived in a humans' place, but there weren't any human people there."

"The thing I do like about the sea," said Rudi, who

Accidents

wasn't really listening, "is the way it goes on and on. Look, if you come a bit further down the path - now look out into the distance."

Benjamin's jaw dropped as he looked out - and away and away further to the horizon, and for the first time saw the shining blue expanse of sea seeming to stretch out to the end of the world.

"Now that is impressive," he said.

"Good, isn't it? When we go away on tour, we go across that in a boat."

"Really?"

"Yeah. It's dead scarey, the boat goes up and down all the time over the bumpy bits."

"Waves," said Tonya absent-mindedly; she was thinking about something else. "Ben, what d'you mean, there weren't any people there?"

Benjamin didn't answer, and Rudi said: "Cats often live in empty houses, what are you on about?"

"I think you should tell us your whole story," said Tonya firmly. "We're your friends. And then we can say we know where you've come from and all about you. Come up off the path, look, there's a sunny bit up there."

They made their way to the patch of sun higher up in the woods. Rudi pounced at a beetle which came out from under some dead leaves.

"Missed," he said.

"I used to practically live on those," said Benjamin. "You have to be quick."

They settled down on the brown leaves. "Start at the beginning," said Tonya.

9. BENJAMIN'S STORY

"You have to understand about my mother," said Benjamin. "Mam was exceptional, in the same way you circus artistes are, she had a talent. Well, she was very clever all round, really, but she was brilliant with numbers, she could do anything with them.

"She was born on a farm in Wales, her parents were the farm cats. She said she remembered it was a good life, lots of food, they could do as they pleased...

"The farm human people were no trouble, they were mostly working. They used to have other humans that came there for their holidays, and two of these saw her when she was still a kitten and they realised how clever she was, and they asked if they could take her away as a pet. So they took her to a town quite a long way away."

He paused a moment; as always it was difficult to talk about his mother. "They were a man and a woman, young. They had a cybercafé, d'you know what that is?"

The two circus cats stared at him blankly.

"D'you know what a computer is?"

"Sort of," said Rudi. "It's a machine, isn't it?"

"Yes, well, they have a thing called the Internet where all the computers can talk to each other even across long distances."

"Like Auntie Anastasia," said Tonya. "We had this

old auntie, she could tell what was happening to other cats in the family miles and miles away. Specially if it was something bad, she was very gloomy. But she couldn't always do it, she had to be in the mood."

"The computers can always do it, " said Benjamin, "but not all the human people own one, so the cybercafé is a place where they can use a computer and the Internet, and meet other human people."

"You wouldn't think they'd need places to meet," said Rudi. "There's millions of them all over the place, all they've got to do is stand still and they bump into each other."

"They want to meet ones that they'd like," said Tonya, "don't be silly."

"So all the people who came to the cybercafé liked my Mam, and made a fuss of her, and she watched them using their computers, and she worked out how to do it. She said it's pretty easy if you've got small paws. And of course, you have to be able to read some of their language because on the screen it tells you what to do."

"You've lost me," said Rudi, "I thought the thing with a screen was a television."

"It's like that only different."

"D'you mean your mother could actually read human language?" Tonya was impressed. "I thought only the ancient cats of Mau could do that, I didn't think anyone could nowadays."

"No, there are cats that can. Well, I can actually, but not as well as my parents could. It's getting easier because the computers put a lot of things in little pictures rather than words. So anyway, she learned how to work the computer and she used to have fun after they'd all gone to bed, it's called surfing the net."

"But surfing's what they do on those boards. On the sea."

"Don't try to understand human stuff, Rudi, none of it makes sense," said Tonya.

"But then this ... this bad cat found out the things my Mam could do. And he took her and made her work for him."

"How d'you mean, took her?"

"Some cats that worked for him just grabbed her and made her a prisoner and took her away to where he was."

There was a rustling in the leaves nearby. All three cats turned instantly, ears pricked. But it was just a handsome, unwary blackbird rummaging about for worms. He suddenly saw the cats and fluttered straight up into a tree, shouting the blackbird alarm call: *chink - chink - chink - chink !* at the top of his voice.

"That's done it," said Rudi.

A dozen other blackbirds took up the cry and in a moment the whole wood was echoing with the piercing sounds.

"Oh, shut up," said Tonya. "We're not hunting you, we're having a private discussion."

CHINK - CHINK - chink - CHINK - CHINK - CHINK - chink - chink - chink!!!

"Look!" Rudi called out, pointing to his stomach. "Well fed! Not hungry! No threat to blackbirds!"

CHINK - CHINK - CHINK - chink - CHINK - CHINK chink - chink!!!

"Let's get out of here," said Tonya.

They made their way back to the path, pursued by the blackbirds who flew over their heads, shouting at them.

"This is a nice wood you've got here, " Rudi called out to them. "We were enjoying it. Can't we all just get along?"

The blackbirds took no notice - their noise was so deafening now that the three young cats broke into a run. Only when they reached the end of the path and came back out into the lane did the birds leave them alone and they could hear the *chink chink*s quieten down and then stop.

"We weren't doing anything," said Rudi crossly.

"It's no use once they start like that, they just go mad," said Benjamin.

"Didn't they do it to you, when you lived in the woods?"

"No, they knew I was rubbish at hunting, they didn't take any notice of me."

"So how did your Mam get from this bad cat to the woods? What did he make her do? When did you arrive?" Tonya was really involved in Benjamin's story.

"You don't have to tell us if you don't want to," said Rudi.

"Yes he does. Come into this field, look, it's quiet here."

They slipped under a gate into the field. Rudi said if the cows started shouting at him he was going home. The field was rather full of cowpats, but they found a clean patch of grass and settled down again.

"I don't want to talk about the bad cat very much," Benjamin said. "But while she was working for him, my Mam met my Dad. He was being made to work too, same as her. So they fell in love and I got born.

"But they wanted to get away. My Dad ran away, he was supposed to go to the farm in Wales, Mam told him to go there and wait for her. Then later on, Mam and I got away too, but Jack and Tabbyfoot were sent after us. We were on our way to the farm, but we had to hide in the woods and then..."

"We know what happened next," Tonya said hastily.

"So your Dad could be living at the farm now?" Rudi said, surprised. He'd never thought about Benjamin having a father.

"If he got there, yes, he could be."

"Didn't you try to go there and find him?"

"I didn't want to lead Jack and Tabbyfoot to him. They'd have killed him too. So I stayed in the woods, till the circus came along."

"Wouldn't you like to go and find him, I mean if it was safe?"

"I'd like to see him again and know he's all right. But I want to stay with the circus now. If I can."

Tonya and Rudi were silent for a while. It still wasn't the whole story, but it was clearly all Benjamin was going to tell them today.

A cow was grazing quite near them, lifting her head every now and then to chew and stare at the three young cats with no expression at all in her huge brown eyes. Then she lifted her tail and deposited a huge smelly cowpat on the grass.

"Charming," said Rudi.

"S'pose we'd better be getting back," said Tonya.

It was even hotter and more thundery as Benjamin, Tonya and Rudi wandered slowly back up the lane.

Rudi stood up on his hind legs to swipe at a small blue butterfly, but it quickly fluttered out of his reach. Tonya felt sleepy; she was glad they didn't have a show that night - they would be moving on to the next pitch. Benjamin was walking a little ahead, lost in his own thoughts.

They were turning a corner in the winding lane, nearly back at the circus pitch, when Benjamin stopped and ducked back into the grass at the roadside.

"Get back, get out of sight!" he hissed.

Rudi and Tonya dropped down onto their stomachs in the long grass behind him. "What is it?"

"I saw something... Stay here." Slowly, slowly, as if he were creeping up on a beetle, Benjamin inched forward until the bend in the lane showed him clearly what he had only glimpsed before.

A big white cat with one tabby foot. And two muscular young ginger-and-white cats. Moving cautiously down the lane towards the circus camp.

They had their backs to Benjamin, but even so he was paralysed with fear for a moment.

Then he moved slowly backwards, not daring to turn round, until he bumped into Tonya and had to half-turn towards her. *"What?"* she mouthed, seeing his expression.

"Tabbyfoot. And two others. Going towards the circus."

"They didn't see you?" Rudi whispered.

"No. But they could come back this way any minute. We've got to get off the road."

It was easier said than done. Each side of the lane was a muddy ditch, and a thick thorny hedge designed to stop farm animals from getting out.

"Go back, back to the cow field," said Rudi, and the three young cats turned and ran as fast as they could back to the gate.

The Russians were much fitter than Benjamin, but he was more frightened - he got to the gate first. They slithered back underneath it and into the field.

They dashed across the open grass to a big iron tank full of water, which they could hide behind.

It was muddy and dirty all round the tank where the cows had stood round it to drink, but the cats didn't care about that right now. They dropped down, exhausted, on the side of the tank away from the gate.

"They'll never pick up our scent with all this stink of cow," said Rudi. Nearby cows looked at them and breathed heavily through their noses.

"How did they know the circus was here?" Tonya couldn't believe it. "We've been miles and miles since the place where they had the fight with Buster."

"I think they've got a spy in the circus," said Benjamin. "in fact I'm sure they have, but I don't know who it is. Buster thinks so too."

"They don't give up easily, that's for sure." Rudi looked at Benjamin. "What d'you want to do, wait here?"

"D'you think anyone saw us leave the pitch?"

"I doubt it," said Rudi. "They were all asleep or practising."

"So with any luck, their spy can't tell them where we are. "

"But sooner or later we'll have to go back towards the circus and they'll be waiting for us. How many did you say there were?"

"Tabbyfoot, and two younger ones, they look like fighters. We wouldn't stand a chance."

Tonya said: "Quite soon, our family's going to wonder where we are. And if they all start running around shouting for us, calling our names, it's going to give everything away. They're going to know we're out here somewhere - and they're going to know you're definitely with the circus, Benjamin."

"I think they know that anyway. All that hiding in shopping baskets and stuff was a waste of time. But you're right, Tonya. You two need to go back without me."

"Yeah," said Rudi, " we should be able to cut through the fields without having to pass too close by them – even if they see us it won't matter. Then we can tell the grown-ups what the situation is."

"As long as no one did see all three of us go off together," said Tonya.

"If they'd known I was out here with just the two of you, they'd have got me by now," said Benjamin.

The three of them thought about that for a moment, then they all stood up.

"Will you be all right?" Tonya looked anxiously at Benjamin.

"Let's hope so. Listen, seriously, tell Miss Kate - I really mean this - if she wants to go without me I'll understand."

"But you're our friend."

"I've brought nothing but trouble to the circus."

"You've brought lots of other things," said Tonya. "You helped Ping, you sorted Maria out. "

"And now we get paid on time," said Rudi.

"I could manage. Those woods looked quite nice. I could eat a few of those blackbirds, that'd shut them up."

"Don't be daft, Ben, of course we won't leave you behind." Rudi gave Benjamin a friendly push with his front paw. "Where will you be?"

" I'll go back into the woods - the place where we were sitting before."

Rudi peered round the tank. There was nothing in the field except cows. "Right," he said. "Good luck."

"Good luck."

The two young Russians ran swiftly away across the grass. Benjamin watched their silvery shapes disappearing under another gate into the next field.
Then he drew a long breath, and keeping low to the ground he set off in the opposite direction.

10. BACK IN THE WOODS

Benjamin realised with surprise that he had grown. Only a short time ago he could have slid under the brambles and pretty much buried himself in the dead leaves of the woodland floor; now it was much harder to be invisible. Buster's insistence on regular exercise and plenty of good food was having the desired result.

He settled into the patch of woods where they had been earlier. The patch of sun had gone now, but it was still a pleasant little clearing. *I just hope those blackbirds don't start up again.* But just as they had done before, in the other woods, they seemed to take no notice of him. *It's like they know that I'm being hunted, I've become prey too.*

Sitting there in the woods alone, crouched like a small dark big-eared lion, Benjamin felt suddenly angry. *I'm not going back to those days. I'm not going to eat beetles and live in fear. Why should I? Somehow I'm going to get away from them and be a free cat. Somehow.*

"Well," declared Miss Kate firmly. "I'm afraid that's it. We've done all we can for Benjamin, he's a very pleasant young cat as far as I can see, but the circus doesn't need all this nonsense of cats following us and stalking around. It's bad for business. If he's said he's happy for us to leave him behind, that's what we'll do."

"He didn't exactly say he'd be happy," said Rudi.

"I'm sure he'll manage. There are some houses around here, he can adopt some humans and get them to look after him."

Tonya and Rudi said nothing. Buster looked serious. They were outside Miss Kate's van, and she was sitting on the steps, neat and elegant as ever, but perhaps a little tense and speaking a little louder than usual.

There was a short silence. Miss Kate briefly washed her left shoulder.

"Right," Buster said. "Things to be getting on with."

He and the two young Russians headed across the dusty, flattened grass towards their caravans; almost at once they met Maria.

"Have you seen Benjamin?" she asked them. "I can't find him anywhere."

"Benjamin has left the circus," Buster said.

"He's WHAT??" Maria screeched at the top of her voice. "He *can't* have! He's my best best friend, he wouldn't have gone without saying goodbye."

"We all know he's had some problems and there's been some unpleasantness since he's been with us. He offered to leave, and Miss Kate thought it would be best to let him go."

"I don't BELIEVE it!"

"That's the way it is," said Rudi abruptly.

Maria stared at Rudi and Tonya, her eyes round and furious. "Is that all you've got to say? I thought you were supposed to be his great buddies, we can see how much that's worth, can't we!"

"Maria," said Buster severely. "You're a circus cat born and bred. You don't need me to tell you that cats come and go, it's how we live. Benjamin isn't an artiste like you, he's just a cat who's travelled with the circus for a while, and now we're going our separate ways, that's all there is to it. Now stop making such a noise."

He walked rapidly away and bounded up the steps into his caravan.

"We couldn't do anything about it," said Tonya. "Miss Kate made up her mind." Avoiding Maria's outraged gaze, she turned away and headed for the Russians' caravan, followed by Rudi.

"He never said goodbye to me!" wailed Maria. "What am I going to do without him?"

She ran into her caravan and burst into tears. Her loud howls could be heard all over the circus camp.

The circus cats began packing up their equipment and their daily belongings, stowing everything away in its usual place in the vans and trucks. Everyone was rather quiet.

Maria stomped from her caravan to the big tent to fetch her coloured ribbons, and stomped back again with an expression that dared anyone to speak to her.

Back in the caravan, Tonton looked at her as she put the ribbons away. "He'll be all right," he said quietly.

"Oh will he? And what about *me*? He's the only friend I've ever had."

Tonton smiled wryly to himself and packed up the food dishes.

It was growing dark in the woods. Benjamin still sat under the trees in the same place.

Cat Circus

He was starting to face the fact that the circus cats might have taken up his offer to stay behind, that they might even now be packing up to leave without him. It would be the sensible thing for them to do. Miss Kate had her whole circus to think of, not just him.

Maybe no one would come to fetch him. No cheerful Russians, no big friendly Buster. He would have to take on the world alone once more.

With Tabbyfoot and her two sidekicks still in the neighbourhood.

Tonton glanced around the caravan. "Right," he said. "I'm just going to have a quick word with the Nagas. And I'll check what time we're leaving - in about an hour, I should think. D'you want a snack before they clear the food tent?"

"No thanks, I'm all right."

Tonton left the caravan.

Maria sat on her bed and counted to a hundred. Then she got down, went to the door and looked cautiously out.

The hunter-drivers were busy taking the food tent down. Everyone else was in their caravans. She could hear loud voices from the clowns' van as they had another argument.

Maria went silently down the steps from her caravan, took another quick look around and trotted towards the edge of the circus pitch.

They might not care about Benjamin, but she did. She wasn't going to leave him behind out there somewhere. She was going to find him and persuade him to stay with the circus.

Back in the Woods

With a defiant wave of her grey tail, Maria left the pitch and set off across the darkening fields.

Benjamin watched the moon climb higher above the trees. He knew there was not long now before the circus would leave.

In spite of himself, a small sad mew came out of his mouth. He must try not to think about them, try to forget the happy evenings crammed into the Russians' van while they sang songs and told stories, try to forget sharp, kind Miss Kate, try to forget Buster who always looked out for him but never fussed...

Benjamin felt awful. His earlier defiant mood had completely vanished, he felt that he was turning back into the tired, frightened little cat with the big ears who had nothing to look forward to but hiding and despair.

He hunched down into the dead leaves and waited for what the night would bring.

Maria's sense of smell was pretty good even for a cat, and she quickly found the lane and realised that Benjamin, Rudi and Tonya had all been this way some hours before.

She ducked into the grass and paused for a moment, seeing one of the hunters in the lane talking to some other cats who were probably from the farm. After a short time they finished their conversation and went off in opposite directions. Maria emerged and got back onto the scent of the three friends.

She tracked them back to the gate into the cow field, peered under the gate but could see nothing in the dusk except cows settling down for the night. She hesitated, then put her nose down again and picked up their scent on the other side of the gate.

She followed on down the lane and into the woods.

There! she thought. *He's just in here somewhere. I'll find him and make him change his mind, and we can be back before it's time for the circus to leave.*

"Benjamin!" she called. "Benjamin, are you here?"

One of the blackbirds made a tut-tutting noise from its nest overhead.

Maria put her nose down again and trotted along the woodland path.

Up in his hiding place, Benjamin had been in a kind of miserable half-sleep. He thought he heard someone calling him, but he wasn't sure.

Suddenly there was a crackle of broken twigs, a flurry of dry leaves, and a mass of grey fluff bounced on top of him.

"THERE you are!! What are you doing lurking here? I knew I'd find you, silly Benjamin off on your own!"

It was Maria, pushing her nose into his in a big sloppy kiss.

"Maria, what, Maria what are you doing? Are you here by yourself? Where are - sssh, stop making so much noise. Maria, *shush!"*

"Why? What's the matter?"

"Those bad cats are after me again," whispered Benjamin, " that's why I'm here."

"Oh, I know that. That's why Miss Kate said they were going to leave you behind."

"Is that what she said?"

"She said you wanted to leave the circus, but you don't, do you? Come on, come back now and we'll persuade them. It doesn't matter about those bad cats, they won't get you."

"Ah, but that's where I'm afraid you're wrong, my dear."

Benjamin's fur stood on end all over his body. He turned his head slowly in the direction of the chilly voice.

The big white cat Tabbyfoot stood a few feet away, looking at them with an amused expression. The two ginger-and-white toms were approaching them from the other side. One of them was carrying a coil of rope. There was no escape.

"My, young Benjamin Mew," said Tabbyfoot. "How you've grown."

"Leave him alone," said Maria. "What's he ever done to you?"

"Deal with her," said Tabbyfoot.

In an instant the two tomcats leaped at Maria - but she was even quicker. She flung herself at the nearest tree and started climbing. The two hunters dashed up after her.

Benjamin started to his feet, but was felled by a single blow from Tabbyfoot. "No, no, my gallant young friend. No coming to the rescue of the fluffy damsel. You stay on the ground where you belong." She pinned him down by one powerful paw on his neck and another on his rib-cage. He could hardly breathe.

But Maria, the high wire artiste, was climbing up and up the tree, into smaller and smaller branches which swayed and sagged under her weight. One branch nearly gave way and she jumped like a squirrel to another one.

One of the tomcats lost his footing and slipped halfway down the tree. The other one paused. Maria was up in the topmost twigs now.

"Leave her," said Tabbyfoot. "She doesn't matter. Let's get young Master Mew back to the marmalade factory."

The two tomcats half scrambled, half fell back down the tree, and landed next to Tabbyfoot, who had neatly tied Benjamin's paws together.

They took a large stick from the ground nearby, put it through between his paws, the two tomcats put the ends of the stick on their shoulders and carried him away, trussed up like a shot tiger.

"Good night, Miss Impertinent," Tabbyfoot called up to Maria.

"You'll never get away with this," Maria shouted back. "We'll find him. We'll hunt you down. No matter how long it takes. You'll regret the day you hurt a cat from the Kochka Circus."

"How very dramatic. Seems to me the Kochka Circus is rather glad to get rid of him."

And Tabbyfoot loped swiftly away through the woods. From high up in her tree, Maria could just see the pale shape of the big female disappearing along the dark path.

A cold gust of wind suddenly swept across the trees. The twigs swayed and bent, Maria clinging on in the darkness.

"Benjamin!" she shouted. "Hang on! Don't worry! We'll come and find you!"

But he was too far away to hear.

11. MARMALADE

Some of the circus trucks had already left when Maria ran up the steps of Miss Kate's caravan and barged straight in.

Miss Kate, Buster and Tonton were all in the van. As they saw the panting Maria, who had bits of twig caught in her fur and mud all over her paws, they looked even more serious than they had before.

"I was just telling Miss Kate you'd gone missing," said Tonton. "What have you been up to?"

"They've taken Benjamin, the bad cats, they've taken him away!"

"They've got him?" Buster looked at Miss Kate. "You were right, we left it too long."

"They're going to make him into marmalade! You have to do something," Maria wailed at Miss Kate, " you CAN'T leave him behind!"

"Marmalade isn't made out of cats, Maria, it's made out of oranges. And we were never really going to leave Benjamin behind. The idea was to announce to everybody that we were going to, so that their spy would hear it and tell them. Then we would pack up and go, and later on Buster would double back to fetch him, and we hoped that way we'd shake them off. But I was afraid they might find him first."

"I should have known it was too risky," said Buster. "But Rudi and Tonya said he had a good hiding-place."

"It was the best idea we could come up with at the time," said Tonton.

Maria's eyes got suddenly even rounder. "Oh, no... I must have led them to him. I saw three cats in the lane, but I didn't know who they were, I thought they were from the farm. Then I tracked Ben and the two Russians down the lane into the woods, and almost as soon as I got there, the bad cats arrived."

"If you could track him so could they, don't blame yourself."

Maria gasped as she remembered. "The first time I saw them, they were talking to one of the hunters."

"Which one?"

"It was Rip."

Even tied up and miserable as he was, Benjamin still noticed how much smoother a ride it was in Tabbyfoot's car than in the makeshift circus vans. The vans were made out of bits and pieces; Tabbyfoot drove in the most expensive toy car that human money could buy, designed for rich children and improved by skilled cat mechanics with access to unlimited supplies of engine parts. If it had been just a bit bigger she could have taken it on the motorway. As it was, it was covering the miles of minor roads at an impressive speed.

Tabbyfoot was purring as she drove. One young ginger-and-white tomcat was in the front, the other in the back with Benjamin.

Benjamin shifted to try and ease the pain of the rope cutting into his legs. "Stay still," said the tomcat next to him, and hit him hard with his claws out.

"I wouldn't try anything with Jimmy and Joseph, if I were you," Tabbyfoot said. "Your friend the circus strong cat killed their brother."

Both the tomcats hissed, and the one in the front seat leaned over and raked his claws across Benjamin's back. Benjamin let out a yelp of pain.

"You remember Jack?" Tabbyfoot continued. " Of course you do. He was involved in the unfortunate death of your foolish mother. What a lot of trouble Bella did cause. What a lot of time we've spent chasing her and then chasing you. Quite pointless. As they say in the human movies, you can run but you can't hide."

The tomcat in the back seat dug a claw into Benjamin's ear and pulled. Benjamin tried not to cry out again, but he couldn't help it.

"You can do what you like to him," Tabbyfoot said. "As long as it doesn't affect his memory."

Rip was innocently checking the tyres on Buster's caravan, when he was seized by an enormous ginger right paw and thrown roughly to the ground. Then the huge ginger left paw gave him a powerful thump to the head.

Sprawling on the ground, he could hardly see past the looming bulk of Buster to where Miss Kate stood close by. Two pairs of green eyes were staring at him in fury.

It was obviously no use to deny anything. "What's all the fuss about?" he muttered sullenly. "That Benjamin, he's only been here five minutes."

"He's part of the circus. And you sold him to strangers." Buster gave Rip another cuff round the ear.

"I needed the money, right? I lost a lot betting on

rat races. They came round and asked me if I'd seen him, and I had seen him when I went into your van, he was under the cushion but his tail was sticking out. So I said what's it worth, and they gave me more than I owed, just for watching and telling them what was going on. And I set up a few little accidents so he'd get the blame."

"How much did they pay you?" asked Miss Kate. She sounded calm, merely interested.

"A hundred silver." Miss Kate nodded thoughtfully; that was more than four weeks' wages for Rip. "And I'll get more," he continued defiantly, "when I go and work for them full-time."

"If you believe that, you'll believe anything," she said. "They've got what they wanted out of you."

"You had a good job here, a career, why throw it away?" Buster couldn't understand.

"No, I didn't. Sam and Ted and Martha run everything, they just tell you what to do, fetch this, get that, bring us in another dozen mice, I'm sick of it."

"But we all have to do that when we start out -"

Miss Kate interrupted Buster; she saw no point in having a discussion. "You're a very stupid young cat, and now we're going to go, and leave you behind. You can fend for yourself and see how you like it. You can go and see your nasty friends in - where was it?"

"Plymouth," said Rip, and then wished he hadn't.

"In Plymouth, thank you. I'll be very surprised if they offer you anything but the door. Goodbye."

Miss Kate turned and walked away. Buster gave Rip a punch in the ribs as a parting gift, and followed her towards her caravan.

Sam got into the driver's seat of Buster's van and started the engine. He didn't speak to Rip or look at him.

Marmalade

All the remaining circus vans started up and drove away towards the lane.

The chilly breeze carried the quiet chugging of their engines away from Rip as he sat and watched them go. It was as if his old life was leaving him silently, in a dream.

"If I hadn't bet on that bloody white rat, none of this would have happened," he said.

"I trusted him," said Buster crossly. "I thought he was a really good young cat, coming on well, promising future with the show..."

"There'll always be some cats that let you down," Miss Kate said. "Think of all the times you've had faith in someone and you've been right. " She pushed a bowl of pilchards across the table in her neat van. "Help yourself, Buster."

"Thanks." Buster took several large mouthfuls, which seemed to calm him down. "I hope," he said as he wiped his mouth with his immense right paw," I hope you feel we did right to trust Benjamin."

"I'd hardly have let him do the accounts for the whole circus if I didn't trust him," Miss Kate replied with a slight edge to her voice. "As far as I'm concerned, Benjamin's one of us and we must act accordingly."

"So they're from Plymouth, that explains why we didn't leave them behind. We've been travelling towards their territory not away from it. Ben should have told us that."

"He was very young when he and his mother ran away, he probably doesn't remember what direction they went in. It's a pity he didn't tell Rudi and Tonya any more. We still don't really know what we're up against here."

"All the Russians'll help, and young Maria, probably Tonton and the Nagas too. The other artistes aren't so friendly with him."

The hunters should be keen to make up for what Rip's done."

"What we need now," said Buster, " is a plan."

Tabbyfoot drove her car into the garage on the ground floor of the marmalade factory, drove past the two gleaming full-size limousines and right up to the lift.

She got out, climbed quickly on top of the car and leaned over to press the lift button: the doors opened at once and she drove the small car into the big factory-sized lift.

"Going up to the top?" asked the tomcat next to Benjamin, as he climbed up to reach the buttons inside the lift.

"Oh yes," said Tabbyfoot.

The lift glided upwards. Benjamin knew that there would be a human porter on duty in the entrance hall on the ground floor , but he would be unaware of the lift moving as the cats had long ago disconnected the indicator lights. Anyway it would be the night porter and he was probably watching television, as the man had been when Benjamin and his mother slipped past the desk and out of the front door which was propped open. That, too had been a hot August night.

The lift stopped on the fourth floor and the doors opened. Tabbyfoot drove the car out onto the wide landing and parked it.

The tomcats dragged Benjamin out of the back seat.

"We can cut him loose," Tabbyfoot said. "He's not

going to escape again."

One of the toms fetched a knife and sawed rapidly through the rope. Benjamin tried to stand up but couldn't. The two ginger-and-white toms pushed and pulled him through the big double doors into the penthouse.

It was exactly how he remembered it - a big, wide room with huge sofas, deep-pile carpet, dimly lit except where groups of cats in brighter pools of light were gambling on various games, chatting, watching television. In other rooms they would be sleeping or eating smoked salmon, caviar - whatever Joe had provided.

None of the cats looked round as Tabbyfoot came in. She didn't like being stared at.

She walked straight through the first room and into a smaller, but even more luxuriously furnished room.

"Tell Joe I'm here and I've got Bella Mew's son," she said abruptly.

A young cat scurried through a door. Seconds later he reappeared and nodded.

Tabbyfoot walked over to the door - several cats got out of her way - followed by the two toms and Benjamin, who could just about walk now.

At the door she stopped, the two tomcats let Benjamin go, and she scratched on the door, pushed it open and dragged him with her inside the gloomy room, leaving the toms outside.

"Well done," said a voice which Benjamin remembered.

It wasn't an unpleasant voice like Tabbyfoot's. It was extremely ordinary. That was the thing about Joe Bloggs: he was the most ordinary cat you could imagine. Just a normal tabby with a bit of a white shirt-front, average size, average weight. Everything average, except his extraordinary air of calm confidence. Nothing ruffled Joe Bloggs. He had it all under control.

He sat on the enormous desk in the dark library with its rows of books and big leather chairs, the only light coming from the reading lamp next to him, and looked down at Tabbyfoot and Benjamin.

"It took a while, but still, well done," he said. "Get up on that chair, what was your name? Benjamin, that's it."

Obediently Benjamin climbed up onto the big chair. Tabbyfoot stood by, on guard.

"It was a shame about your mother, but she brought it on herself. You understand why it had to be done."

Even bruised and captive as he was, Benjamin felt a surge of anger and bitterness. "Yes. You thought she knew too much. But what danger was she to you? Who could she have told? She wasn't exactly going to walk into a human police station and tell them the whole story, was she?"

Tabbyfoot hissed briefly at his tone, and Joe Bloggs looked at him thoughtfully.

"You've become quite an assertive young cat while you've been traipsing around with that circus. That may not be an advantage in your present situation. Obviously, neither you nor your mother could have conveyed to the humans what we do here - but you could teach other cats, couldn't you?"

"I suppose so. I haven't met any who'd be any good."

"And there remains the question of the Swiss account numbers. Your mother was the only one who had access to those numbers, but I'm sure she told them to you. Didn't she?"

Benjamin said nothing.

Marmalade

"Of course she did. So there was nothing to stop you setting up in business on your own."

"How could we have got the computers?"

"I'm sure sooner or later you would have found a way. Bella certainly would, if she'd lived. And I can't allow other cats to be 'queering my pitch', isn't that the circus term? So of course, knowing what you know, you have to be here with us. Or you have to be dead. The choice, as they say, is yours."

There was a long silence.

Then Benjamin said: "I suppose I'm here with you, then."

12. THE CATS OF MAU

The circus was travelling on, and in the Russians' caravan Rudi and Tonya were feeling miserable. They knew that Miss Kate and Buster hadn't given up on Benjamin, but with each day that went by it was harder to believe anything could be done to rescue him.

Now they were on the road, all the Russians crowded into the big van, apart from Dimitri and Sasha who were driving.

Little Vladimir suddenly said, "I miss Ben."

"We all do," said Vera.

Tonya didn't want to get into a discussion about her lost friend, it made her want to howl. Hastily she said: "Mama, tell us about the ancient cats. How they got the humans to teach them things."

"Yes!" said Vladimir. "I like that story because the cats win. And Tasha doesn't know it yet."

Olga settled herself more comfortably on her cushion, and began. "In the ancient times," she said, " the humans in the land of Mau built great buildings and they studied mathematics and the movements of the worlds in the sky. The land of Mau is hot and dry, but they found ways to move water around the land so that it became green and they could grow crops. Corn was very important to them, they ate it themselves and sold it to other people.

"They kept the corn in great storage buildings, but they reckoned without the mice, which got into the stores and ate huge amounts of it. Not only did they eat, but being dirty little mice they also - "

"- peed on it!" said Vladimir.

"- pooed on it!" shouted Tasha.

"- so that much of the corn was spoiled and had to be thrown away. The well-fed mice had more and more little ones until there were more mice than there are drops of water in a river. The cats of Mau thought they were in heaven. They chased and caught and ate to their hearts' content. But of course, they were wild cats and they came and went as they chose.

"More and more of the corn was becoming dirty and worthless, and the people were afraid they would be poor and have nothing to eat. So the wise men of the Mau approached the leaders of the cats and said: 'Come and live in our houses and in our corn stores, and we'll take care of you. You shall have meat and fish when we have it. You shall sleep in a sheltered place. Foxes and wild dogs will no longer trouble you. All we ask in return is that you kill the mice, which is what you like to do anyway. Doesn't that sound like a good deal?'

"And the cats said: 'To you, maybe. But we know we can find food and shelter all by ourselves, and the foxes and wild dogs don't bother us, we're too quick for them. What else can you offer us?'

"The wise men had no answer. They thought of the cats just as animals who wanted only food and safety.

"The cats said: 'We want your cleverest men to teach our cleverest cats the things you know about mathematics and the movements of the worlds in the sky.'

Cat Circus

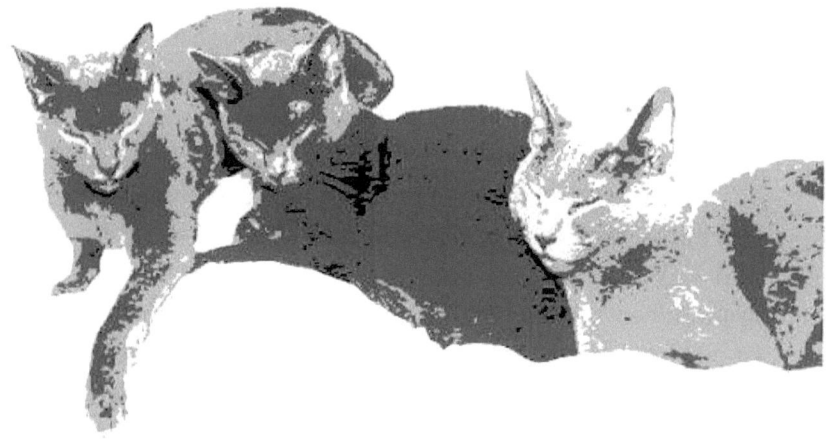

Listening to the story

'Do you really?' said the wise men, very surprised.

'We want to learn writing, and perhaps a little philosophy.'

'Do you think you're up to it?'

'Try us and see.'

"So the wise men agreed, and the cleverest cats went to live with the cleverest human people; they quickly learned to do arithmetic and to use written symbols, and they acquired most of the knowledge of the people of Mau."

"Why didn't we learn to speak their language, as well?" Tonya asked.

"It's not possible," said her plump aunt Vera. "Our mouths aren't built the same as humans'. Anyway, their languages are so ugly, who'd want to?"

"Meanwhile," Olga continued, " the ordinary cats moved in with human families and got the mouse problem under control.

"The people of Mau were hugely impressed by the cats. They treated them with great respect, and after it had been explained to them about Cat Goddess, they added her to the other gods in their religion, though they would never understand that she is actually the most important of all.

"Centuries passed and the kingdom of the people of Mau ended. Some of their knowledge was forgotten by humans for a long time. The kingdoms that came afterwards had no respect for cats. Their languages were different and very few cats had a chance to learn them. They had no idea of all the things we knew, though some ignorant ones became aware of some things we could do, and thought we must be in league with evil gods. There were some dark times.

"Luckily as time went on they forgot about that idea. And all through the years, to this day, many cats go on living in houses, going out into a garden, being given food, training the humans as far as possible so that things are pleasant and easy. For cats who like it, it can be a very good life."

"Benjamin can read human language as well as ours," said Rudi, "and he can use a computer."

"Really? He was a clever young cat," said Olga.

"Perhaps that's why he had problems with bad cats," said Vera. "There's such a thing as knowing too much, if you ask me."

13. WELL-FED SLAVES

Benjamin pressed his paw down on the left side of the computer mouse. **Please enter your password** said the screen. The man Prendergast had used the same password for everything. Benjamin typed it in, **S-P-L-E-N-D-I-D**, and pressed the mouse down again.

Please choose a transaction. Benjamin chose **Transfer funds.** Then he typed in an account number, and in answer to the question **How much would you like to transfer?** he typed **50,000**. Another click on the mouse, and he had moved fifty thousand pounds of humans' money.

"I've moved that cash over now," he said to the cat sitting next to him.

"Thanks," said the other cat, whose name was Dennis. "I've got a list of more stuff they want - mohair blankets, driftwood sculptures, more cars, where are we going to put it all?"

"No idea," said Benjamin, looking thoughtful.

He stretched, and licked his front paws. Picking out the letters on the keyboard made the ends of his toes sore. Some of the other cats said it was easier if you kept your claws out, but he found that if he did that it still hurt and the clicking noise set his teeth on edge.

He looked around the room, which was in the

second-floor flat. The number of computers had doubled since he was here as a kitten. There was a whole row where cats were busy at the work his mother had started out doing - managing the building, writing letters to the human staff and anyone else like the local council, paying electricity and gas bills.

Everything could be done by email or through a website. It never occurred to any of these humans that the letters they got were not from other people but written by cats. Most of the letters contained the standard paragraph which Joe Bloggs had invented and which answered any questions:

' *According to my dear wife's wishes, the flats are maintained for the benefit of her beloved cats. We are unlikely to meet as I seldom visit the premises myself, however I have ensured that staff and sufficient funds are available to maintain the building in a hygienic and proper manner.*'

The letters would end with a scrawled signature over the name *Felix Nemo*.

Funds certainly were available. Now that Benjamin had told Joe Bloggs the numbers of the Swiss bank accounts, there was another three million pounds.

Benjamin understood now why Joe had been so anxious to have the Swiss bank account numbers. In the next room was a row of brand new state-of-the-art computers, on which several cats were buying and selling stocks and shares.

Big money was being traded, the cats communicating with companies in the City of London where smart young businessmen and women had no idea that the emails and money transfers were coming, not from other people like them, but from small furry animals. One of the cat share-traders had told Benjamin he should try to join them. "It's good fun - it's like hunting, you wait for the right moment and then pounce."

He saw enough to know that Joe Bloggs might be spending a lot of money on furniture and toys and computer games - not to mention the two large Mercedes cars in the ground-floor car park, which he would go down and sit in from time to time - but he was making money too, a lot of it. Investing, gambling, buying, selling - everything Joe's human, Prendergast, had been doing before he went to jail.

"So your Mum and Dad were, like, in at the beginning of all this?" Dennis, the cat next to him, was intrigued by Benjamin, who saw no harm in answering his questions – though for some reason he avoided telling him anything about the Circus.

"Well, no, the real beginning was the man Prendergast, the one .. Joe Bloggs lived with." They were all a bit hesitant about saying Joe's name: if any supposed lack of respect was overheard by the enforcers, life could get very unpleasant.

"Yes, he got money out of other humans by what's it called, fraud. Promising them stuff."

"He must have been very good at it," said Benjamin. "He had a lot of money. Really a lot. Then he got caught by the police, but for some reason they never found out about this building, or about several of his bank accounts and credit cards. So ... Joe," Benjamin lowered his voice even more, " Tabbyfoot, and a couple of other cats had been living in the penthouse flat upstairs. My Mam said Joe was fond of the man Prendergast, it seems he had found Joe in the street as an abandoned kitten; when the man went to jail, Joe didn't want to leave and find another human. So the cats stayed here. When the food ran out, they got hungry, until Joe thought of ordering some food online, like he'd seen Prendergast do a hundred times."

"It's easy once you know how," said Dennis.

"Yes. He put the internet order through, and the food was delivered to the downstairs door. The porter brought it up to the penthouse and left it outside the flat. As soon as he'd gone, they brought the parcel inside and ate the food. And then he realised. He and his friends could live here in luxury until Prendergast came out of jail, and they could even make him some more money. They could do everything on the internet. No one need ever know they were cats."

Dennis grinned. "Brilliant."

"And then he searched for cats like my parents who had found out about computers and could do the more complicated things, and he brought them here to work for him."

"You've got to admit," said Dennis, "It takes vision. No other cat would have thought of it."

But Benjamin, who had been living with a different kind of cat family, saw, even more clearly now than he had as a kitten, that Joe was a bad cat doing things the wrong way. There were plenty of cats who would have been happy to work for Joe - it was interesting and fun to fool the humans, to eat anything you liked, to laze about all day as many of Joe's hangers-on did - but he ruled by fear and threat. Dennis might pretend to admire him, but really he was just afraid.

Ever since Benjamin's mother, Bella Mew, had run away and Joe Bloggs found out she had been hiding money from him, Joe was terrified that other cats would escape or

Well-Fed Slaves

find ways to steal money, so all the computer operators were constantly watched by Tabbyfoot's gang of enforcers.

Benjamin saw that one of them was looking at him now, so he peered at his screen and pretended to be calculating something. Everything he did would be checked through by another cat when he was asleep. Because they did so much work with humans, most of the operators kept human hours and slept through the night, but there were always guards and enforcers awake.

The problem was that Joe, clever though he was, didn't understand how any of the money transactions worked. He was really bad at maths. But he loved the money, loved the power it gave him to buy things. The apartment on the first floor was full of stuff Joe had ordered; there was a new group of cats now, trying to sell some of it off through internet auction sites.

As Benjamin clicked through another transaction, he wondered for the hundredth time how everyone was at the Kochka Circus. He missed them in a numb kind of way, because he couldn't let himself start feeling how desperate he was.

He and the other computer operators were well-fed slaves; perhaps the share-dealers had a bit more status, but all of them were liable to be bullied, insulted, even beaten up by Tabbyfoot's gang and the smarmy, two-faced cats who hung around Joe Bloggs and pretended to be his friends. And Joe could turn on you suddenly, accuse you of treachery or theft, and you would disappear. Tabbyfoot made no secret of the fact that she had killed cats and enjoyed it.

Bella Mew had found out about Prendergast's secret Swiss bank accounts, but kept the knowledge to herself, and passed it on only to Ben. She thought Joe was continuing Prendergast's crimes, taking money from innocent people, and should be prevented where possible. But once she ran away, Joe had found out about the accounts and the huge sums of money in them.

Knowing the account numbers hadn't saved Bella, but it had saved Ben - he had no doubt he'd otherwise be dead by now. Joe had needed him for that, and now with his accounting skills, he was useful, but other cats could do what he did. And he reminded Joe of Bella, who had been too clever for him.

He had to get away. There must be some way to do it. But he was always watched, even when he was asleep.

The former marmalade factory, four floors high, was joined to another building on one side, and on its other three sides there were narrow streets.

On the ground floor there was the front entrance hall, the lifts, and old warehouse space turned into a big garage area. The floors above had been made into three loft-style flats. Apart from the lifts, there was a fire-escape staircase, a metal one on the outside of the building, but it was closely guarded at all times. There was another staircase, but it didn't go all the way down to the ground floor. Benjamin - especially Benjamin - was not going to get out easily.

When Joe saw Benjamin he talked often about Bella. Ben thought Joe had liked her, even been a little afraid of her, and it was as if he knew that killing her had been unnecessary and evil and he had to keep trying to make out it was her own fault.

But Ben was surprised that Joe never mentioned his father, Edgar, the big thoughtful black cat who had loved Bella in secret, who had made the mistake of arguing with Joe but had managed to run away just before Joe gave the order to kill him.

Had his father ever made it to the farm in Wales? Or was he dead? Surely, if he was dead, Joe would have taunted Benjamin with the fact. Perhaps he didn't know where Edgar was either, and didn't want to admit it.

Certainly Edgar was not as vital to the operations as Bella had been, his knowledge wasn't as dangerous; he had written many of the letters in the early days, hiring the new porters and cleaners, because his English was particularly good, but there were soon other cats who could do the same work.

Benjamin was determined to get out, to rejoin the circus, and maybe one day to find his father. But how?

At least he could be ready, if ever there was a chance to get away. Dennis slipped off for a toilet break. Benjamin glanced around and then clicked onto a new page. **List all accounts?** it asked. Benjamin clicked **Yes.**

14. THE CIRCUS COMES TO TOWN

The night porter said "Take care, mate, cheers," and put the phone down. He was a young Australian and had taken over the job at the old marmalade factory from a friend of his. It was a complete doddle, his friend had said, nothing to do all night and you can make all the international phone calls you want.

That certainly made up for the inconvenience of working nights, though it was a weird job all right: the letter of appointment had been in funny old-fashioned English and signed by some bloke called Nemo. He yawned, found some beach volleyball on the satellite TV and leaned back to watch.

Some time later he got up to fetch a drink from the small kitchen off the main entrance hall. As he passed the glass double doors, he saw a cat outside, a grey long-haired cat, very pretty, with a long fluffy tail.

The porter opened the door. "What're you doing out here?" he asked. "All you guys are usually upstairs. Living in pampered luxury. Did you get out by mistake?"

The fluffy cat wound herself round his legs and purred.

"D'you want me to take you up in the lift?" He walked towards the lift, but the cat got in the way. Then she stretched up and put her paws on his knees and miaowed softly.

The porter reached down and picked her up. She cuddled into his arms and purred. "Well, that's a first," he said. "I've never had any of you lot talk to me before. Come and sit with me and watch the telly, eh?"

Still holding the cat, he went into the kitchen and fetched a couple of cans from the fridge, then sat down back at the reception desk and put his feet up. Immediately the pretty grey cat draped herself over his stomach, purring away and kneading his sweatshirt with her paws.

"You keep those claws in, now," said the porter, pulling the tab off one of the drink cans.

He completely failed to notice four small, oddly shaped vehicles driving past the doors.

Seeing that the night porter was now fast asleep, Maria jumped lightly off his chest and went over to the glass doors. She leaned against one of them to push it open: but it was much too heavy to be moved by one cat. She pushed again, and again.

Outside the doors, cats began to emerge from the darkness and gather in a group, more and more of them. Maria made a final effort and got the door open a crack. Instantly, strong paws were thrust into the gap and, pulled by three or four big hefty cats, the door swung open enough to allow them all to dash through - Sam, Ted the Ear, Martha, three of the other hunters, and then all the Russians.

Suddenly the entrance hall was full of cats, silent, purposeful, running fast towards the two lifts at the back.

The buttons to call the lifts were about one and a half metres off the ground, but the Russians were already forming their pyramid, without the springboard so Sasha and Dimitri had to pick up the younger ones and sort of throw them up onto the waiting backs. In no time at all, Vladimir was at the top and triumphantly pressing the button.

Maria watched anxiously, glancing from the cats to the sleeping porter as the doors of one lift glided open.

The hunters dashed inside - and the pyramid of Russians, still in formation, shuffled inside too with Vladimir still at the top, ready to press the button inside the lift.

Maria jumped back onto the night porter's desk as the lift doors closed, Vladimir waving to her as he disappeared from view.

Just as she settled back on the porter's chest, he stirred and woke.

"Still here, then, girlie? Good on you. I've had girlfriends left sooner than you." He stroked Maria's head, and she purred loudly.

The porter looked sleepily around. Hall, doors, street outside, everything was quiet.

The lift doors opened on the first floor, and the circus hunters came out cautiously, ready for trouble.

Outside the lift was a big landing, and then double doors going into the first floor loft apartment. The doors were open, and beyond them all that could be seen was a lot of boxes.

Sam, Ted the Ear, and Martha moved on silent paws into the loft. Suddenly there was a surprised miaow, quickly muffled.

Moments later, Martha came back to the waiting

Russians and the other hunters, gathered on the landing.

"That was easy," she said quietly. "Just a couple of guards and they were asleep. Looks like this is a storage area."

The rest of them followed her, past boxes and crates and piles of expensive rugs and cushions.

"Those big white boxes smell of food," Rudi whispered to Tonya.

"Those are fridges," Dimitri murmured. "They keep the food cold so it lasts longer."

"Neat idea," said Rudi.

"Over here," Sasha called quietly. He had found what they were looking for - the door to the fire escape.

It was the kind of door that can only be opened from inside, with a heavy bar that has to be pulled down.

Igor and Irina, Rudi and Tonya looked at each other and swiftly lined up in front of the doors. Dmitri whispered "One..two..three..jump!" and the four young cats leaped up and hooked their front paws over the bar. Their combined weight was just enough to pull the bar down - but it made a loud clanking noise and all the circus cats froze where they were for a moment, listening.

There was no sound from upstairs. The door was slowly pulled open from outside, and out on the fire escape was the huge form of Buster, with Miss Kate's slim black-and-white shape just behind him. They stepped inside, Sam propped the fire doors open with a box, and all the circus cats headed back towards the lifts.

"Now you young ones wait here," Buster said. "If there's any trouble, any fighting, you don't go to investigate, understood? You go out of those doors and down to the vans."

"Can't we do the lifts?" Tonya asked.

"We don't need you to," Miss Kate said. "Look, on this floor there's a chair placed so a cat can reach the button." She jumped up and pressed the button as she spoke. The doors of the second lift opened. "And there's another chair inside this lift, it must be the one the cats use. You've done very well, now stay here - and keep hold of Vladimir."

Even as she was speaking, the older cats were all crowding into the lift. "Don't let those guards get out, " Martha said. "They're in a sack over by the window." The doors closed, leaving Rudi, Tonya and Vladimir behind.

"That's not fair," Tonya said," Benjamin's our friend."

"It's scarey down here," whispered Vladimir.

"Let's have a look in those fridge things," said Rudi.

On the second floor, Benjamin was asleep on the bench near his computer, when something woke him. What was it? He looked around.

Most of the computer operators were asleep. Only a few cats who were trading in stocks and shares on markets across the world were still crouched in front of their screens, and a couple of checkers were looking through some emails that other cats had sent. They didn't seem to have noticed anything, but the guards had heard something - the ones by the lift and the ones by the fire doors were wide awake.

Suddenly the lift doors slid open and a mass of cats came hurtling out. Benjamin gasped as he recognised the older Russians and some of the hunters, and he leaped from the bench as he glimpsed Buster, Sam, Ted and Martha still in the lift before the doors closed again.

Instantly, Joe's guards attacked the new arrivals and the loft was full of squalling, fighting cats, kicking, biting, locked together and rolling over and over, crashing into the furniture.

The computer operators, wide awake now, cowered under their desks in terror.

Ben ran towards Dimitri who had just knocked one of the guards clean out with a blow from his muscular paw. "Dimitri, Dimitri, it's me!"

"Ben, there you are!"

"These cats don't matter, all the bad ones are upstairs."

"We thought they might be – come on!"

Vera, Olga and Irina were dragging the operators out from under their desks and herding them into corners, dealing out nasty scratches to anyone who resisted.

Dimitri headed for the lift, but Benjamin said, "There's a staircase on this floor, here -" and led him towards the narrow back stairs. There were more guards there, fighting viciously with Sasha and Igor.

From up in the penthouse came the sounds of wild fighting and breaking glass.

"Ah, sounds like the Nagas have got there," said Dimitri.

As Benjamin and Dimitri reached the penthouse level, they saw a scene of complete chaos.

The Naga Family and Tonton had just swung down from the roof outside, on ropes with bricks attached, breaking the windows and then scrambling neatly through the holes in the glass. Now they were opening the fire escape doors to let in the rest of the circus hunting team, who were immediately set upon by guards and enforcers.

Buster, Sam, Ted, and Martha were fighting their

way through from the lift. Though Tabbyfoot's gang were violent cats, they had no discipline or training, and the fit, strong circus cats were able to beat them - but not easily. Blood and fur were flying through the air.

Many of Joe's hangers-on were already heading for the fire escape doors or the stairs; a couple of really nasty cats who had always been hateful to Benjamin nearly knocked him down in their haste to escape. He tried to trip them up but wasn't quick enough.

The noise was deafening. There was an ear-splitting screech from Tabbyfoot as Buster threw aside two guards and charged at her, knocking her sideways. She ripped at him with all her claws at once. They locked together in a screaming, spitting ball, biting and kicking at each other.

Where was Miss Kate? Where was Joe Bloggs? Benjamin dodged through the battle to try and find them, knowing they were the only ones who could stop the fighting.

He found them both. They were crouched a metre apart on the huge desk in Joe's library, poised, tense, staring at each other, backs arched, low growls of hatred rumbling in their throats.

"Joe," shouted Benjamin. "The humans'll have called the police! They'll have heard the noise! It's all over."

For a fraction of a second Joe continued to snarl at Miss Kate, and then his quick brain took in what Ben had said, and he suddenly relaxed his stance, shook his ears and smiled at Miss Kate. She was completely taken aback.

"Sorry to deprive you of this encounter, dear lady," said Joe. "But survival is always the better option." And before he had finished the sentence he dashed like lightning out of the door.

Benjamin heard him shout to Tabbyfoot: "Get out,

Tabs! Leave him!" and heard Tabbyfoot screech back: "The only way I'll leave this one is in his grave!" before she was silenced forever by a terrible bite from Buster - and Joe disappeared out of the fire escape door into the night.

"Good to see you, Ben," said Miss Kate, and to his surprise she gave him a quick kiss.

"Miss Kate, I've got to do something downstairs - and there's a lot of stuff on the first floor, the circus could use some of it, cars and things - but we must hurry, the humans'll come soon!"

The night porter was out at the front of the building, talking on his mobile phone. "I don't know, I just heard a whole lot of the windows go and the cats are going mad up there. Yeah, cats, the building's full of 'em. I'm not going up there on my own, it must be a gang or something. Look, are you going to send somebody round or not?"

He looked up at the front of the square four-storey building with the faded words painted on the front: MURLEIGH'S MARMALADE Est 1889.

Windows had been broken on the top floor. Cat yells and screams were echoing through the air. "Sounds like they're killing the poor creatures," he said.

"What're you doing?" asked Irina, who was still guarding the terrified computer operator cats.

Benjamin rapidly found the document he was looking for. He copied it into an email, addressed the email to: fraud@plymouthpolice.co.uk, and pressed **Send**. "Just something I prepared earlier. You can let these cats go, they won't do any harm."

Cat Circus

The female Russians backed away from the operators, who certainly didn't seem capable of any resistance.

"Come on, come with us," Benjamin called over to them. "Dennis?"

Dennis shook his head, putting his ears back at the sound of crashes and yowls continuing from up in the penthouse.

"Come on. All this is over now. You can be free."

"Never mind them, Ben, let's get out of here. Rudi and Tonya are downstairs."

"Right, now listen, downstairs - "

In the very early morning, Rip was limping towards the marmalade factory. He had walked all the way from the place where he and the circus had parted company, keeping himself going with visions of the life Tabbyfoot had told him about: smoked salmon, caviar, mohair cushions, and some serious gambling action.

He turned the last corner - and saw, in the dawn light, three police cars and two RSPCA vans parked in front of the building, and six or seven humans, some in uniform, standing by the cars talking between themselves or into mobile phones.

A female RSPCA officer came out of the building holding a large cat carrier. Several cat faces peered angrily out through the wire mesh; one had quite a lot of blood on its ear.

A human was saying into his mobile phone: "I haven't a clue what's been going on here, but it's over, that's for sure."

"Oh, *rats*..." said Rip.

15. CELEBRATION

"Well, Ben," said Miss Kate, settling back on the cashmere blanket which now adorned the bed in her caravan. "It's extremely pleasant to have you back. And all the things that we... acquired from the marmalade factory will be very useful, especially the model cars, we can use them for spares and get these vans into better condition."

Benjamin nodded happily.

"It was clever of you to remember the things we might be able to use. Obviously you were thinking a lot about the Circus?"

"Oh, yes."

"And you'll be staying permanently with us now?"

"Oh, yes, please."

"Good. Good." Miss Kate seemed to be waiting for something; Benjamin didn't know what to say. He had been at a loss for words for quite some time.

There was a quiet cough from outside the caravan.

"Ah," said Miss Kate. "I think we should go over to the food tent now."

Buster was waiting for them outside the van - the marks of his battle with Tabbyfoot all cleaned up and hardly visible under his thick ginger fur - and as Benjamin walked across to the food tent between the two older cats, he thought he couldn't possibly be happier.

Cat Circus

He was wrong.

As they went into the tent, a cheer went up, music began, and he saw that every cat in the Kochka Circus was there, from tough old Sam to Lily and little Tasha, all smiling and applauding him and waving their tails.

And spread out in front of them, the biggest meal he had ever seen, all the goodies from Joe Bloggs's downstairs fridges, and more. Salmon, caviar, sardines, finest Mediterranean pilchards, roast chicken, duck, Scottish grouse, pheasant, guinea-fowl, fresh mouse, fresh goldfish, eggs, milk, cream, little savoury biscuits with butter on, and great bowls of the finest spring water.

The tent was decorated with brightly coloured ribbons and streamers, and the musicians were playing away like mad.

"Hurray for Benjamin!" shouted Maria.

"Double hurray!" shouted Tonya and Rudi.

"Treble hurray from ME!" shouted Vladimir.

"You're going to see something now," said Buster. "In the Kochka Circus, when we celebrate, we celebrate! Welcome home, Benjamin."

The End

www.ingramcontent.com/pod-product-compliance
Ingram Content Group UK Ltd.
Pitfield, Milton Keynes, MK11 3LW, UK
UKHW041436180426
11947UKWH00007B/474